Oh, yes, she needed this job—a top-of-the-tree job working for Vasilii Demidov as his PA on a six-month contract that carried a salary that made her catch her breath.

It was nearly twice as much per month as she had been earning, plus it would open doors for her and enhance her CV—not to mention distance her from the present calamity in her career.

The fact that she had recently been on the internet again, looking up Vasilii Demidov, meant nothing other than that, like any candidate for a new job, she wanted to arm herself with as much knowledge about the business for which she hoped to be working as she could. And in the case of Vasilii Demidov's business, Vasilii himself *was* the business.

Everything she knew about Vasilii Demidov suggested that he was a man who was immune to the kind of vulnerabilities experienced by the rest of the human race. A powerful, hardheaded man, who was completely focused on the success of his business. Not the kind of man who was likely to welcome the knowledge that a fourteen-year-old had had such a huge crush on him that she...

That was enough!

Laura checked her watch and quickened her walking pace. She must not be late for this all-important appointment—and she definitely must not be late because she was daydreaming about the man who would be interviewing her.

Penny Jordan

THE POWER OF VASILII

RUSSIAN RIVALS

TORONTO NEW YORK LONDON
AMSTERDAM PARIS SYDNEY HAMBURG
STOCKHOLM ATHENS TOKYO MILAN MADRID
PRAGUE WARSAW BUDAPEST AUCKLAND

Recycling programs
for this product may
not exist in your area.

ISBN-13: 978-0-373-23793-7

THE POWER OF VASILII

First North American Publication 2011

All about the author...
Penny Jordan

PENNY JORDAN has been writing for more than twenty-five years and has an outstanding record—more than 165 novels published, including the phenomenally successful *A Perfect Family, To Love, Honour and Betray, The Perfect Sinner,* and *Power Play,* which hit the *Sunday Times* and *New York Times* bestseller lists. She says she hopes to go on writing until she has passed the 200 mark—and maybe even the 250 mark.

Although Penny was born in Preston, Lancashire, U.K., where she spent her childhood, she moved to Cheshire as a teenager, and has continued to live there. Following the death of her husband, she moved to the small traditional Cheshire market town on which she based her Crighton books.

She lives with her Birman cat, Posh, who tries to assist with her writing by sitting on the newspapers and magazines Penny reads to provide her with ideas she can adapt for her fictional books.

Penny is a member and supporter of the Romantic Novelists' Association and the Romance Writers of America —two organizations dedicated to providing support for both published and yet-to-be-published authors.

Books by Penny Jordan

Harlequin Presents®

2969—GISELLE'S CHOICE**
2999—A STORMY SPANISH SUMMER
3023—THE MOST COVETED PRIZE*

*Russian Rivals
**The Parenti
Dynasty

Other titles by this author available in eBook

CHAPTER ONE

SHE really should not be doing this. She really shouldn't.

It was a job—that was all. A job she needed now, thanks to what had happened, and needed badly.

A job working closely with Vasilii Demidov. Very closely. As his temporary PA, in fact. Mid-stride, Laura Westcotte stopped walking along London's Sloane Street.

Oh, for heaven's sake.

She wasn't fourteen any more, and in the grip of a massive crush on the very grown-up and breathtakingly, spine-shiveringly, far too excitingly male older half-brother of one of the new intake of day pupils at the school where her aunt was the matron and she'd been a pupil by virtue of her aunt's post, was she?

No, she wasn't.

Nor was she still the same silly girl who had secretly and eagerly searched the internet for every scrap of information she could find about Vasilii Demidov, committing to memory every single piece of information she'd managed to find about him. Thank goodness the big social networking sites hadn't existed then, for her to make a total public fool of herself with, Laura thought wryly. Snatching that photograph of him to daydream over in private had been bad enough.

She'd taken it when he had come to the school to collect his half-sister one Friday afternoon. Her hands had been trembling as she'd watched him walk from his car to where his half-sister had been waiting for him, the muscles of his male body moving so powerfully beneath their covering of denim jeans and a black tee shirt that the sight of him had made her go hot with longing. It was a wonder that the resultant photograph hadn't been so blurred as to be unrecognisable. She had hidden the print in her most sacred of special places: the 'secret' drawer of the jewellery box that had originally belonged to her mother, and which had always somehow held an echo of her mother's special scent. She still had that jewellery box.

And the photograph?

Now she was being ridiculous. *If* she did then it was simply because she'd never thought to throw it away. No other reason.

She had been such a very young and idealistic fourteen-year-old that worshipping from afar had come as naturally as breathing.

She had woven such ridiculous fantasies about the two of them meeting—the kind of fantasies that only an over-romantic, lonely girl with her hormones burgeoning into reckless life could weave. In her imagination she had even allowed herself to believe that because they had both lost their mothers there was a special bond between them.

All that and she had never even come face to face with him properly, never mind spoken with him. She had, though, dreamed endless daydreams about him, torn between an aching longing for him to notice her and the thrill of fear she had felt at the thought of that happening, and how she would cope with that level of sensual excitement.

So what? That had been then. This was now. She had just mentally said his name several times without her heartbeat going into fifth gear and then overdrive, hadn't she? No, she wasn't fourteen any more, Laura assured herself. But she still couldn't stop herself from glancing into the window of the expensive designer shop she was hurrying past on her way to her interview, as though she needed to reassure herself that the reflection she could see there was that of an assured twenty-four-year-old woman, and not a fourteen-year-old girl. A woman, moreover, whose brunette hair swung sleekly and under control to her shoulders, and whose blue-green eyes in her heart-shaped, Celtic pale-skinned face, like her soft full lips, were discreetly made-up—as befitted a careerwoman about to undergo an interview for a job upon which her immediate financial security depended.

So why the need to check? Surely she didn't *really* fear that somewhere within her that lonely, overly idealistic and romantic girl she had once been still existed, and that by some dangerous alchemy Vasilii Demidov could resurrect that girl and her crush on him just by the mere fact of them breathing the same air?

Instead of thinking about the past she should be focusing on her own present, Laura reminded herself. To mangle that famous Oscar Wilde quote, to be rejected and dismissed for one job for which she was well qualified might be overlooked as merely unfortunate, but to be rejected for a second would be a bad mark against her that would lie on her career history for a long time to come.

She was under no illusions, of course. She knew exactly why she hadn't been given the verbally promised promotion in her previous job. The reasons had, after all, been made more than clear to her by the company's new CEO.

The pain and humiliation of what she had undergone momentarily drove the colour from her face.

Oh, yes, she needed this job—a top-of-the-tree job working for Vasilii Demidov, as his PA, on a six-month contract that carried a salary that had made her catch her breath. It was nearly twice as much per month as she had been earning, plus it would open doors for her and enhance her CV—not to mention distance her from the present calamity to her career.

The fact that she had recently been on the internet once again, researching Vasilii Demidov, meant nothing other than that—like any candidate for a new job—she wanted to arm herself with as much knowledge about the business for which she hoped to be working as she could. And, in the case of Vasilii Demidov's business, Vasilii himself *was* the business.

And what a business. Vasilii had taken charge of the business portfolio originally begun by his late father and had turned it into a multinational empire. The head office of this empire might technically be located in Zurich, but from what Laura had been able to learn the reality was that the head of the empire still adhered to the traditions of the Nomad desert warriors of his maternal family. He travelled almost continuously between all the places in which he had business and financial interests.

Unlike so many other Russian oligarchs, Vasilii did not own lavish homes all over the world. Instead he stayed in hotel suites or concierge apartments, as though at heart his spirit needed to move as ceaselessly as the sands had once moved beneath the feet of the camels in the camel trains of his mother's people.

How intrigued and awed she had been at fourteen to learn that Vasilii, whilst being half Russian through his Russian father, could trace his roots back through his mother's family to one of the most noble and ancient races to travel the deserts and the rugged terrain of the southernmost part of Russia's old territories. There was a legend she had read saying that this tribe of light-skinned and light-eyed desert warriors had once mixed their blood with that of a lost Roman legion, and that their centuries-old pride in their warrior skills came from that time. There had been other stories on the internet about the tribe, and its fierce pride and equally fierce adherence to its own code of honour.

Like so many of the old desert tribes its numbers had been reduced by war and disease long before Vasilii's mother had been born. She had fallen in love with Vasilii's father, and then been lost to both her husband and her son in the most tragic of circumstances. She had felt such a surge of idealistic love when she had learned from her aunt the story of the kidnap and subsequent death of Vasilii's mother.

But that had been then, and this was now—and everything she knew about Vasilii Demidov *now* suggested that he was a man immune to the kind of vulnerabilities experienced by the rest of the human race. A powerful, hardheaded man, who was completely focused on the success of his business. Not the kind of man who was likely to welcome the knowledge that a fourteen-year-old had had such a huge crush on him that she…

That was enough!

Laura checked her watch and then quickened her walking pace. She must not be late for this all-important appointment—and she definitely must not be late because she was daydreaming about the man who would be interviewing her.

From his exclusive concierge apartment on the top floor of one of London's most prestigious hotels, Vasilii had an excellent view of Sloane Street and the surrounding neighbourhood as he stood at the window of the apartment's smart boutique-hotel-style sitting room. A shaft of late July sunshine falling across his face threw into relief the harsh scimitar-sharp angle of his cheekbones and the taut line of his jaw.

To his Russian compatriots the golden warmth of his skin and the autocratic boldness of his nose might mark his genes as those of an outsider—someone who belonged more to the Arab world than their own—but he had grown up just as much of an outsider to the world in his late mother's family as he had his father's: truly accepted by neither, marked physically by his mother's genes and mentally by his father's brilliance as a businessman. An outsider who had learned young to walk alone and to trust no one other than himself. Especially after his mother had been kidnapped and then murdered by her kidnappers in a rescue attempt that had gone wrong.

To have been as emotionally dependent on his mother's love as he had been as a child, and then to lose that love, had taught the man he had become the necessity of protecting himself against such vulnerability. And that was exactly what he had done, holding other people at a distance and promising himself that he would never allow himself to become vulnerable to the pain of love and loss again.

Right now, though, it wasn't the past that was making him frown, it was the present. The present and a certain Miss Laura Westcotte.

If it had been unfortunate that his PA had had to take compassionate leave for six months to be with his sick wife, then it had been irritating that the temp hired to take his place had gone down with a particularly vicious form of the norovirus bug—just when Vasilii had been at the most delicate state possible of negotiations with the Chinese, and thus most in need of a PA who was not only fluent in Mandarin but also in Russian, and of course English, and who understood the protocol and etiquette complexities of negotiating with high-ranking Chinese dignitaries and officials. Vasilii might be fluent in all three languages himself, but one of the things one did not do when negotiating with high-status Chinese officials was risk losing face or, even worse, risk causing them to lose face by doing one's own translating.

Vasilii had quickly discovered that when dealing with the Chinese the existence of an impressive retinue of personnel was extremely important. Which was why right now he was waiting to interview Laura Westcotte, the applicant best qualified to suit his needs according to the headhunters he had hired to find someone.

However, there were excellent reasons why Laura Westcotte was *not* the applicant or the PA Vasilii wanted. The first was that she was female—Vasilii never took on female staff to work closely with him. He had quickly learned that female graduates were far too likely to see him—unmarried and extremely wealthy—as potential husband material, and Vasilii had no intention of getting married—ever.

A muscle flickered in his jaw, as though he'd had to tense his body against a surge of unwanted emotion. Marriage, like any close relationship, meant giving something of yourself to others. It meant commitment, and it meant being vulnerable to loss and thus to the most terrible pain.

The contradiction within him that came from his dual heritage meant that living alongside the modern Russian was a fierce desert warrior, whose handed-down moral code and beliefs were hopelessly out of step with modern-day life. And why should he marry? There wasn't any need. His half-sister Alena's recent marriage to a fellow Russian meant that in all probability there would at some stage be children from that marriage, to work for and take over the family business in due course.

But it wasn't just his aversion to having a female PA that made him antagonistic towards having Laura Westcotte as his PA. Despite her impressive CV, what he'd learned about her through Alena, along with the investigations he'd had made about her, proved she lacked both responsibility and ethics, and therefore could not be trusted. In short, morally she was everything he did *not* want in his PA. Unfortunately, though, there was no other applicant for the post who was anywhere near as well qualified for it.

It wasn't just that her Mandarin and Russian were, according to all the enquiries he had made about her, beyond compare, it was also that her grasp of the manners and customs of both the modern-day-business and diplomatic Chinese worlds was so nuanced as to be in a class of its own. Those skills were exactly what he desperately needed right now if he was to secure the Chinese contract he had been pursuing for the last fifteen months. Not to secure it wouldn't just affect his business empire and its profits, but also its future growth potential

No, he had no other choice. He would have to offer Laura Westcotte the job.

It was the incredibly swift upsurge of the lift that was responsible for the unwanted fluttery sensation in her stomach, and not the thought of coming face to face with the man who had been responsible for those embarrassing to remember feverish teenage fantasies and romantic daydreams, Laura assured herself as she waited for the outer door to Vasilii Demidov's serviced apartment to be opened. This was a job interview she was attending, after all—for a job she desperately needed, she reminded herself. She simply could not afford to show any kind of nervousness—no matter what the cause. Given what she had read about Vasilii's ice-cold clinical ability to slice through anything that stood in the way of his targeted business goals, he was obviously not someone who would be sympathetic to uncertainty or nervousness in others. He was far more likely to use that vulnerability to his own advantage.

The clicking and whirring of internal locks accompanied by a mechanically controlled voice instructing her to 'enter when the green light shows' had Laura stepping as confidently as she could into a marble-floored rectangular inner hallway brilliantly lit by concealed modern lighting.

A pair of double doors off the hallway opened automatically, and a disembodied voice from within the room beyond them commanded curtly, in an upper class English accent, 'Come.'

It was hardly the warmest of welcomes, Laura recognised as she stepped towards the doors and then through them, into the smartly modern room beyond. Her attention, though, wasn't focused on the expensive designer furniture and decor of the room. Instead it had flown like a homing pigeon to the man standing in front of one of the room's two tall balconied windows, with his back to her.

Like her, he was wearing formal business clothes—a dark suit. His equally dark hair just touched the white collar of his shirt. His hands, which were at his sides, were tanned and ring-free. His head was angled slightly to one side, so that the light from the window caught the sharp bone structure.

The flutters she had felt in her tummy when she'd got out of the lift had turned into a distinct and discomforting curl of sensation—not, of course, awareness of him as a man, and certainly not helpless female appreciation of that maleness. That could not be allowed to be possible. Not with the very personal knowledge she had of herself and the way other people might translate it were they to know. It wasn't as though she had actually *chosen* to be that way. And it certainly didn't have anything to do with Vasilii Demidov and those teenage feelings she had had for him.

What she was feeling was simply a very natural anxiety, Laura insisted to herself. Professional anxiety because she needed this job so desperately. That was all.

And then he turned round.

The man her fourteen-year-old self had adored must have been stored in her memory in soft focus, and that focus had been gentled by idealism, Laura acknowledged, torn between wishing that there was a chair for her to steady herself on and being glad that there wasn't as she withstood the searing, biting hostility of a gaze that felt like the coldest wind that had ever blown off the winter steppes.

She had taught in Russia for a while, just as she had in China, whilst studying the languages of both countries, and she knew exactly how that wind could burn into one's flesh and senses, destroying those who weren't strong enough to withstand its onslaught.

That wind and the whip of desert sand and its burning heat had surely carved the bone structure of this male face that was stripped of all softness. The tanned flesh might look velvet-warm, and human enough to tempt any woman's yearning touch, but the flint-grey eyes warned of the fate that would destroy anyone reckless enough to attempt the forbidden intimacy of doing so. That this was a man who prided himself on not having any human vulnerabilities within his make-up, Laura already knew from her research, but seeing the reality of all that delineated so clearly and harshly in his features was still a heart-jolting shock. His tall, broad-shouldered frame might be clothed in what looked like the best that Savile Row could produce, but it was abundantly clear to Laura that beneath those twenty-first-century clothes lay not vulnerable flesh but instead a hardened steel armour.

This man had the heritage of both his mother's people's blood and his father's business success soldered into him and onto him. His already critical scrutiny told Laura that. He might by his blood be of the desert, but there was a coldness about him—an air of distance, almost a total rejection of his own humanity allied to a contempt for the vulnerability of others. The sheer onslaught of the information being relayed to her by her own senses was almost too intense for her to manage.

Every warning system her body and her mind possessed was telling her to turn and leave, to run if necessary. And yet…that frisson of sensation, that unwanted but determined sensual awareness of him as a man that trembled through every nerve ending and tingled every pore of her skin meant— Meant nothing. And if it did exist, and wasn't merely something ridiculous left over from her teens, a product of her imagination, it should be ignored, Laura told herself firmly.

* * *

The photograph of her on her CV hadn't revealed the female delicacy and the perfection of her heart-shaped face and its features anything like as clearly as the reality of Laura in the flesh, Vasilii was forced to acknowledge as he studied the young woman standing in front of him. Intriguingly—or suspiciously, depending on your mindset, and his always veered towards the suspicious—she had no internet presence. No unseemly photographs of university antics, no gossipy posts to reveal any real aspects of her personality. But of course he didn't need them. He already had a direct insight into exactly what kind of person she was. The kind he most despised.

She might be physically attractive, and she might have dressed her elegantly slender five feet nine inches in a smart, businesslike, summer weight off-white dress, over which she was wearing an equally smart mid-grey jacket, accessorised with mid-height grey leather pumps and a workmanlike black leather bag, but he knew the reality of her. Just as he knew that beneath the clothes that discreetly skimmed her body she had the kind of curves that most appealed to the heterosexual male's desires, and that they were entirely natural.

Inside his head Vasilii discovered that he was making an illogical and totally unnecessary calculation as to the number of months it had been since he had last cupped the full softness of a woman's breasts in his hands whilst he slowly kissed his way from her throat down towards them. Her skin would be creamy pale, a sensual incitement all of its own to the man who wanted her. But he of course was not that man. He controlled his own male reactions. They did not control him. The powerful lightning strike of sexual awareness jolting through him meant nothing. It was merely an instinctive physical reaction. Nothing more. He had far more important things to think about than the brief, inconvenient surge of male desire, both inexplicable and undesired, that had surged through him.

Turning away from her, Vasilii reached for some papers on his desk, demanding curtly as he turned back, 'I see you speak Russian as well as Chinese? Why Russian, when most Russians who need to speak and understand English already do so?'

His question caught Laura completely off guard, and made her feel self-conscious. She could easily remember how her desire to learn Russian had been fired, and by whom, but she could hardly tell him that it had been the thought of speaking to him in his own language that had motivated her all those years ago.

'My parents were linguists. They both spoke

Russian, and I started speaking it myself, picking it up from them. I thought… I felt… It seemed natural to follow in their footsteps.' It was in part the truth, after all—even if she was not telling him the whole of that truth.

'You decided to follow in their footsteps rather than strike out and make your own path through life? Is that what you mean? Wouldn't you say that that shows a lack of self-determination and ambition?'

'No, I wouldn't,' Laura defended herself firmly. He was deliberately trying to make her feel uncomfortable, she was sure, but she wasn't going to let him. 'Certain abilities do pass down through the generations, after all. In your own case you followed your father into the same line of business, and your success has proved that you have an aptitude for it. I had an aptitude for languages. After I lost my parents, developing that aptitude and those skills and following in their footsteps helped me to feel that they continued to be a part of my life. I loved languages, and I wanted something I could hold on to that felt as though it was part of them.'

Something to hold on to. An image of his mother the last time he had seen her alive flashed briefly and harrowingly through Vasilii's head before he could deny it. The fact that it had been there at all only increased the dislike and rejection he felt towards Laura. She was stirring up within him memories she should not have the ability to stir up, raising issues that no one was ever allowed to raise with him, crossing lines that no one was permitted to cross with her conversation about her parents and her foolish sentimentality. Why? And, even more importantly, how? It was absurd that a woman like her, whom he already knew he could not trust, should somehow have managed to breach the defences that not even the gentle, loving touch of his late stepmother had been allowed to breach. Absurd and dangerous. The day that a woman like Laura Westcotte could represent any kind of danger whatsoever to him would never come, Vasilii assured himself.

'I asked you for an explanation of why you chose to learn Russian. I expected a business reason, not a self-indulgent description of your childhood emotions.'

The harshness in his voice made Laura want to recoil from it—and from him. She'd felt so sorry for him when she'd learned how he'd lost his mother. She'd even felt as a girl that it gave them a shared bond. Was that why she had mentioned her own parents? Did she still want to create a shared bond with him? No! There wouldn't be any point, because no woman would ever be allowed to share any kind of bond with the man he actually was, Laura suspected.

His criticism had stung, and under normal circumstances—if she hadn't needed this job so badly—it would have had her questioning whether he was the kind of person she wanted to work with. She might need this job, but she certainly wasn't going to allow his comment to go undefended.

Straightening her shoulders, she told him spiritedly, 'I may have chosen Russian for personal reasons, but my decision to learn Mandarin—which was *not* one of my parents' languages—demonstrates that I was looking towards the future of business. My parents passed down to me an ability to learn languages, but I made the decision to study Mandarin based on my awareness of the growing importance of China in the world market.'

She was daring to challenge him? That wasn't something Vasilii was used to at all. Not from anyone and especially not from women, who were normally all too eager to court and flatter him.

'You attended the same school as my half-sister. As far as I am aware Mandarin was not on the syllabus there.'

He *knew* she had been at school with Alena? A mental image of herself trying to find out from her aunt when Vasilii was likely to come to the school to collect his sister and then positioning herself at the window that would give her the best view of his arrival flooded her body's defence system with guilty self-consciousness. He couldn't possibly know about that—just as he couldn't know how often she had mentally rehearsed walking oh, so casually past his stationary car as he waited for Alena, only to have always lacked the courage actually to do so. She was being ridiculous, Laura warned herself. Of course he would know that she had been at school with Alena, just as he would know that her aunt had been the matron there, because—naturally, as her prospective employer—he would have checked up on her.

'No. Mandarin wasn't on the syllabus,' she agreed.

One dark eyebrow lifted in a manner that Laura felt was coldly censorious.

'Private lessons must have been an added expense for your aunt.'

He really did not like her. Laura could tell.

'I paid for them myself,' she informed him, her voice every bit as cold as his had been. 'Some of the private pupils stabled their horses locally, and I worked at the stables mucking out. They got an extra hour in bed every morning and I earned the money to pay for my Mandarin lessons. Oh, and before you ask me, I saved up and bought an old bicycle so that I could cycle to the stables.'

Against his will Vasilii had a mental image of a much younger version of Laura Westcotte—ponytailed, fresh-faced and determined—setting off on her bicycle every morning, no matter what the weather, in order to do the chores that girls from better off families were too indulged by their parents to want to do, before returning to the school to begin a day's education. His own father had always insisted that he work for his spending money as a boy, and even Alena, protected though she had been, had had her own special chores to do.

Vasilii pulled himself up. He wasn't used to thinking about other people with his emotions, never mind mentally linking their situation to his own. Quite how and why it had happened he had no idea, but he did know that it must and would not happen again.

'I would like you to read these notes aloud to me, translating them into Mandarin as you do so,' he told Laura, firmly dismissing the unwanted image of her as a teenager from inside his head.

Very quickly Laura scanned the first paragraph of the technical data she had been handed. As an employee of a business specialising in handling translations of and negotiations for highly complex business operations she had become very much at home with the kind of thing Vasilii had asked her to do, so there was no reason whatsoever for her hand and then her whole body to tremble slightly, or for the colour to come and go in her face—apart, that was, from the fact that Vasilii's hand had brushed her own as he handed her the piece of paper. That was ridiculous. Vasilii's touch couldn't possibly have made her feel like that.

She took a deep breath and started to translate the information on the printed page.

She was good, Vasilii was forced to accept as he followed Laura's translation. His own PA would have taken longer, despite his experience.

'And now if you would translate it into Russian?'

Laura nodded her head.

Again she was word-perfect. Not that Vasilii would have expected or accepted anything else.

'So, we have established that your translation skills are…adequate, but if you know anything about China you will know that there is far more to successful business negotiations with the Chinese than merely having a good grasp of Mandarin.'

'Yes, of course,' Laura agreed. 'Even if they speak another language the heads of Chinese industries and high-ranking Chinese officials often use a retinue of interpreters and PAs because that adds to their status. It is part and parcel of the Chinese way of doing business. Since I know that you speak both Russian and Mandarin yourself, I assumed that it was in part because of the issue of respect that you have decided to negotiate through someone else yourself.'

'That is correct,' Vasilii replied, and then looked at her, his eyes slightly hooded and his grey gaze unreadable.

Instinctively Laura knew that his silent assessment of her was both critical and meant to unnerve her.

It would have been so much better, so much easier for her, if she didn't have that silly teenage crush lodged dangerously in her emotions. Its mere presence was enough to weaken her self-confidence.

When the silence instigated by Vasilii stretched to a length that was beginning to feel uncomfortable he delivered the blow that came from a direction she had not been prepared for. 'You resigned from your previous employment,

I understand—without having secured another post first. Why? It is rather a risk in today's financial climate.'

CHAPTER TWO

LAURA felt her heart still in fearful recognition.

He couldn't know. It just wasn't possible. Summoning all her courage, she told him, 'I decided to take a sabbatical,' keeping her tone light and her head held high.

'Really?'

The cynical look he was giving her warned Laura that he didn't believe her. But worse was to come when he continued.

'I understand that you are buying your current property with a mortgage, and that in addition to that financial commitment you also help to pay the fees for your aunt's sheltered accommodation?'

'Yes,' Laura was obliged to confirm. 'My aunt brought me up after the death of my parents. She's not been well recently, and only receives a small pension, so naturally I want to do what I can to help her.'

'You seem very eager to draw a picture of

yourself as someone who takes her duties and
responsibilities seriously, yet your attitude towards job security, which I would have thought
in the circumstances would be extremely important to you, suggests the opposite. In fact I'd
go so far as to say that I find it hard to believe
that someone with your financial commitments
would even think of taking time out for a sabbatical. And I have to say that I find it even
harder to believe when I know that you made
that decision within a month of being offered a
promotion for which you had been personally
selected by your mentor—a mentor with whom
you have worked for many years.'

Laura's heart had started to beat with heavy,
hammerlike blows of acute dread.

There was nothing he wanted to do more than
tell Laura that he had another far more suitable,
far more acceptable applicant to fill the vacancy
as his PA, Vasilii acknowledged as he watched
her, but he couldn't. Her translations had been
faultless and skilled, and he already knew from
her CV how highly her previous employers had
rated not only her negotiating skills but also her
people skills. As Vasilii knew, they were going
to be very, very important in securing this particular contract. However, he intended to let her
know he was not a man she should cross.

Laura could see that Vasilii was waiting for

an explanation, but she couldn't tell him the truth. Instead she had to appear casual and calmly in control, even if she was sick with anxiety inside, and tell him, 'The new position I was offered would have entailed a relocation to New York. I resigned because I preferred not to go.'

'Because you don't want to travel? But the position as my PA involves a great deal of travelling—and to places rather more far flung than New York.'

Laura's earlier anxiety had become a clawing sense of impending disaster. Her dread was justified when Vasilii announced, 'If there is one thing above all else that I demand in my employees, Ms Westcotte, it is honesty and trustworthiness.' He paused, and then demanded, 'Isn't it the truth that you were offered the option of leaving your previous employment voluntarily or being dismissed, because of your affair with your immediate—and affianced—superior?'

'*No!*' Laura denied immediately.

This time it was impossible for her to control her emotions—those feelings that she had kept locked up inside herself since the shocking and humiliating moment when Harold and Nancy had burst into the bedroom of John's hotel room. And then she'd been summoned to

Harold's office to be accused of having an affair with John—her boss and her mentor, a man she loved and admired. A man she looked up to as a career-related father figure. John was, after all, twenty years her senior. He had been divorced when she had first met him, with two sons he adored, and she had been delighted for him when he had become engaged to a wealthy American socialite, a divorcée of his own age whom he had met in New York, even though she had never actually been able to warm to Nancy herself.

One dark, sardonically arched eyebrow told her exactly what Vasilii thought of her hot denial.

'Very well—yes. I *was* offered that choice,' she felt forced to agree. 'But I was not having an affair with John. He was my mentor—a father figure to me in many ways. We were not having an affair,' she stated again fiercely.

'Your CEO thought you were. In fact he was so convinced of it that he offered you the choice of leaving of your own accord, with the whole matter being kept private, or of being subjected to a very public dismissal, with all the damage that would do to your professional reputation. Harold Johnson has very strong views on the morals he expects from those who work under him. He is also an extremely astute CEO, so I doubt he would make such an accusation against a valued and valuable member of his team if he wasn't convinced of their guilt. Was he convinced of *your* guilt, Ms Westcotte?'

Laura exhaled shakily.

'Yes. Yes, he was,' she admitted.

'And he was convinced because he and John Metcalfe's fiancée found you in Metcalfe's bed. Isn't that also the truth?'

'Yes…'

As the excruciating scene came rushing back, Laura could hear in her own voice the dying of her hopes of Vasilii offering her the job. Maybe it was that, or maybe it was the condemnatory look in the flint-grey gaze that right now was clinically ripping her pride to shreds.

Laura didn't know, but something definitely gave her the determination and the strength to insist, 'But it wasn't how it looked. John and I had been working late on a project for a client and the client had taken us both out to dinner, and then a nightclub. There had recently been articles in the papers about young women being at risk in using cabs late at night—especially from nightclubs. We were both tired, and we knew we'd got an early start in the morning, so John suggested I stay overnight in his hotel suite. We'd done it before…'

'Before? Before he had become engaged? When he was a single man?'

'Yes. But…'

'I understand that at the time you elected to share John Metcalfe's suite he and his fiancée were having relationship problems. She had told him that she believed your feelings for him were not those of a mere work colleague.'

'I didn't know about that. John is tremendously loyal. He would never have discussed his relationship with Nancy with me. I had no idea that she had told him that she wasn't happy about the two of us continuing to work so closely together.'

'Because she felt that you wanted to usurp her position in his life and become his wife?'

'That's what she told Harold,' Laura was forced to agree. 'John told me afterwards that she didn't like the fact that he was having to work such long hours.'

'But you, of course, were happy to share those long hours—and his bed.'

'No. I've already told you. John and I were close, it's true, but he was never anything more to me than a mentor and a father figure.'

'You were discovered in his bed.'

'Yes, because he'd insisted that I take it. He slept on the sofa in the sitting room of the suite.'

'A very convenient excuse and one that can't

be proved. Though your willingness to walk away and not fight to prove your so-called innocence speaks volumes.'

Laura closed her eyes. Yes, she had walked away—but only to spare her elderly aunt the stress and upset of watching her niece go through in public what Vasilii was putting her through now.

Vasilii was right in one respect. The fact she had not shared a bed with John could not be proved. But the fact they had never been lovers could—since she was still a virgin. Not, of course, that she was ever going to admit that to anyone—much less *this* man. It was her embarrassing secret. A woman in her twenties who had next to no real sexual experience because… Because she had been too busy with her education. Because she had simply not met the right man at the right time. Never because of that crush she'd had on the man now standing in front of her with such contempt in his gaze. The very thought of ever being challenged to admit that it was because of Vasilii that she was still a virgin, because her crush on him had been so intense that she had simply never desired anyone else with the same intensity, made her feel weak with angry shame.

But that did not alter the fact that Vasilii was wrong about her and wrong to accuse her as he had. She'd chosen to walk away before, but now she was determined to defend herself—and fully intended to do so.

'You obviously want to think that.'

The words were out before Laura could silence them. She wasn't going to apologise for them, though. Not even with Vasilii giving her a look as dangerous as the scimitar swords of his desert ancestor warlords.

'Meaning?' he demanded.

'Meaning that you want to think badly of me,' Laura told him, standing her ground. 'Harold and Nancy's interpretation of what they saw was the wrong one. John and I both told them that, but they didn't want to listen—just as you don't want to listen. You've judged me already, and on someone else's assessment of me. I'd assumed from what I've read about you that you are a man who makes his own judgements rather than a man who runs with the herd.'

Vasilii was hard put to it to conceal his disbelief. Once again she was actually daring to challenge him. She had a certain proud independence about her—he had to give her that. But independence wasn't what he was looking for in a PA.

'I take on board the opinions of others. Who doesn't? And what my own opinion tells me is that so far, despite your excellent CV, nothing you have said inclines me to think that I want to employ you as my PA—a position that demands that the person who fills it is two hundred per cent trustworthy and reliable. You are neither of those things. The accusation made against you in your previous employment proves that you are not trustworthy, and I already know from my own experience that you are if not specifically unreliable then at least not someone who puts duty ahead of their own pleasures.'

There—that should put her in her place and stop her from looking at him with that clear-eyed look of female pride that for some reason made him think about all the ways in which, as a man, that pride challenged him. *All* the ways? Vasilii tensed against the unwanted question. If he was aware of her as a woman then it was only because he needed to assess her so thoroughly. The last thing he wanted was a female PA who was going to create sexual havoc everywhere she went.

From his own experience? What did he mean?

Laura intended to find out. 'What experience?' she demanded angrily. 'This is the first time we have met.'

'In person, perhaps, but I am well aware of the way you behaved when your aunt—who was employed by me to provide my sister with female company here in London—requested you to stand in for her, when she was taken to the hospital. When my sister telephoned you to pass on your aunt's request you decided to go to New York with friends instead—even though you must have known that your aunt was depending on you. In my opinion a person who does not fulfil their obligations to their family is not likely to fulfil those same obligations to an employer.'

Laura's head was a whirlwind of stunned thoughts. This was the first she had heard about any of this. The last thing she would ever do was let her aunt down, and her first instinct was to say as much. But even as she opened her mouth to tell him that she had never at any time received a telephone call from his sister, never mind refused to help her aunt because she preferred to go to New York with friends, she remembered once listening to Alena as a schoolgirl, complaining to her aunt when she had come to the matron's room to ask for a headache tablet that her half-brother was very strict with her, and had advised her parents against allowing her to spend the weekend with another pupil.

'Just because he doesn't approve of her brother,' Alena had protested.

Whilst Laura had sympathised with her, a

small part of her had envied her for having such a protective brother—but then, of course, in those days Vasilii could do no wrong as far as she had been concerned. Now, though, she was old enough to think that Alena might have had her own reasons for lying to Vasilii, and a certain sisterly solidarity was making her feel that she didn't want to betray the other girl—even if that solidarity came at the cost of being misjudged.

After all, what was the point in trying to defend herself when it was plain that he wanted to think the worst of her? Immoral and unreliable—that was what he thought of her.

Surely that wasn't a sharp stab of pain she felt? Why on earth should the biased opinion of a man so condemnatory and arrogant that she already thoroughly disliked him cause her to feel pain? It wasn't pain—it was misery at the thought of not getting the job she needed so much, Laura assured herself.

'Nothing to say?' Vasilii challenged her.

'What would be the point?' Laura asked. 'Since you have obviously already made up your mind about me.' She wasn't going to let him see just how desperately it mattered that she wasn't going to get the job. Lifting her chin she told him coolly, 'I don't see that there is any point in us wasting any more of one another's time. Obviously you don't want me to be your PA.'

'No, I don't,' Vasilii agreed curtly, and paused before adding reluctantly, 'However, unfortunately—given the excellence of your CV in respect of your language and negotiating skills, the inability of any headhunter to find me a candidate to better them, and the immediacy of my need to find a new PA—I have decided on this occasion I have no alternative other than to put to one side my scruples and offer you a temporary contract to cover the next six months. If at the end of that time my negotiations with the Chinese have been concluded to my satisfaction, then in addition to your salary there will be a generous bonus payment.'

Oh, how she longed to be in a position to turn down his offer, Laura thought helplessly. But of course she couldn't. She could tell from his voice how much he resented having to offer her the job. He hadn't let her know that out of weakness or vulnerability. No, he had told her because he wanted her to know just how much contempt he had for her. If she had felt hard done by before, at being falsely accused and then used as a scapegoat for Nancy's unfounded jealousy, that was nothing to the raw, bitter taste of misery she was being forced to swallow down now. She wasn't going to let him think she was grateful, though.

Lifting her chin, she told Vasilii as valiantly as she could, 'Unfortunately for me I have no option other than to accept your offer. But that does not mean that I want to accept it, or that I want to work for you. I don't.'

Their mutual antagonism crackled hostilely on the air between them.

'And just to make things crystal-clear to you,' Vasilii continued, 'whatever your modus operandi or your personal agenda might have been in your previous post, in this one as my PA our relationship will be strictly business. Any woman who thinks that working for me is a shortcut to my bed and via that to a marriage licence will be making a big mistake.'

His bed? For a moment Laura was gripped by panic—had he somehow with some dangerous power managed to learn about her teenage crush? A thousand bolts of searing self-consciousness burned through her. But then her common sense returned. Of course he didn't know. No one had ever known. Not even her aunt. Even so, she wanted to make it clear to him that she wasn't someone who would run after a man—any man, but especially not him.

'Both you and your bed are perfectly safe from me,' she assured him. Unable to stop herself from giving way to her emotions, she couldn't resist adding fiercely, 'You obviously think that you're a wonderful catch, but I certainly don't. If and when I ever marry it will be because I love the man I am marrying and because he loves me in return—because we both want to make a lifetime commitment to be there for one another.'

'A lifetime commitment? No one can or should promise that.'

There was so much anger in his voice—and something else as well that Laura couldn't quite analyse.

As he spoke Vasilii had put down the papers he was holding and had taken a step towards her before he'd even realised what he was doing, never mind understood the reason he was doing it. The experience of letting a woman's jibes cut under his skin—a woman he thoroughly despised and distrusted at that—was so unknown to him that it took him several seconds and several strides in Laura's direction before he could bring his reactions, both physical and emotional, under control.

Even more damaging to his pride was the look of shocked, almost horrified revulsion on Laura's face as she stepped back from him. She was actually raising her hands, palm open, as though to fend him off—as though she was revolted by the thought that he might be going to touch her.

How dared she try to claim the moral high ground? How dared she think she needed to defend herself from his touch after the way he had just warned her off?

Vasilii had a formidable sense of pride, and Laura Westcotte's reaction had virtually flayed it to ribbons. No woman had ever, *ever* reacted to him like that. To Vasilii's angry disbelief, the fact that it should be *this* woman of all women who was rejecting him so obviously, and with such open revulsion, set alight inside him a savage male desire to show her exactly how easily he could punish her for that outrage by making her want him.

The surge of furious and instinctive need for supremacy threatened to slice through all the bindings of modern-day life, convention and even the strict limits he imposed on his own behaviour with such speed that inside his head he was already reaching for her. Reaching for her and holding her, sliding his hands into the lustrous silky warmth of her smooth hair and feeling it glide sensually through his fingers, its tendrils wrapping around them as he bound her to him, a willing captive to the possession of his kiss. Beneath his her lips would part softly and eagerly, clinging to the domination of his.

Her head would tilt back to reveal the vulnerable arch of her throat, her skin as soft as the wing of a white dove at his mother's people's oases. And, as with the powerful life-giving water of those oases, he would be able to slake his own thirst and quench his pride's need for vengeance in the soft sounds of pleasure she would make beneath the sensual punishment of a kiss that would teach her beyond all doubt that she wanted him. He would hear her sigh and sob that wanting beneath his mouth as she pressed herself closer to him, willingly offering herself to him…

The swift aching hardening of his body brought Vasilii abruptly back to reality, away from the dangerous place that his angry thoughts were taking him—in more ways than one.

Thankfully the punishment he wanted to inflict on Laura Westcotte had only been within the privacy of his own thoughts. Naturally he had retained enough sanity not to move so much as a centimetre closer to her, never mind actually touch her—despite the anger she had aroused within him with her obviously deliberately faked attempt to get under his skin by pretending that she was horrified at the thought of his touch. A woman like her would be adept at manipulating situations to suit her own needs.

No doubt she had hoped to provoke him into desire for her after the way he had warned her off. Unfortunately for her she had failed. But at least he had her full measure now that he had himself fully under control, and he would ensure that that control was never compromised again.

As he stepped back from her, though, Vasilii knew that he now had another reason for not wanting to have Laura as his PA. Another reason not to want her. But he had no choice but to take her on.

It was a very galling reality to have to acknowledge, and there was a bitter taste in his mouth as he told her coldly, 'There is no time to lose. My negotiations are at a very critical stage. I have an employment contract here ready for you to sign. Once it is signed I have a résumé of the history of the negotiations so far for you to study, so that you will be up to speed with what has happened.'

'I shall need to know something of the future of your plans, as well as the past,' Laura felt bound to point out.

Now was not the time to allow herself to dwell on the way she had felt when Vasilii had come towards her as though he was going to touch her. It was because she hadn't wanted him to touch her, that was all. Not because she *had.* The very idea was… The very idea was unthinkable.

Taking a deep breath, she continued firmly, 'As you know yourself, Chinese negotiations are very delicate. The wrong pause between words, never mind the wrong look or the use of the wrong word, can set things back far more than we would expect in the West. I know that when someone new joins a negotiating team the instinct is to keep them a little out of the loop facts-wise, until they've proved themselves, but in this instance—'

'I shall be briefing you myself on those aspects of the negotiations tomorrow afternoon, when we shall be flying out to meet the Chinese, once I have assured myself that you have the correct grasp on what has already happened.'

Laura nodded her head. She was very professional when it came to her work, and she had no qualms about her ability to absorb the facts she would need to know. 'Which part of China are we flying to? I only ask because I'll need to pack appropriately.'

'We aren't flying to China. We're flying to Montenegro. Wei Wong Zhang, the head of the company with whom I am in negotiation to work alongside in the development of new modern shipping container ports, has expressed a wish to visit Montenegro. He has other business interests in the potential development of tourist and leisure complexes on China's coast. In the party of officials who are attending will be Wei Wong Zhang's wife, Wu Ying, as well, of course, as the usual government officials and translators. In addition a nephew of Wei Wong Zhang, Gang Li, will also be a member of the party. Gang Li's mother was Chinese-American and he was educated in America. He is very close to his uncle. All the indications are that Gang Li is being groomed to take over the business at some stage. There is, in fact, a suggestion that he might be Wei Wong Zhang's son—although officially that cannot be mentioned and will certainly never be recognised.

'The success of these negotiations has far-reaching consequences for my business that go well beyond the immediacy of this contract. My way of doing business and my status within the business community within China will be judged on my success with this contract. Winning it will by its very nature open doors to further investment in and business with Chinese partners. My PA has prepared a list of the officials who will be accompanying the family to Montenegro. The plan put forward by Wei Wong Zhang, through Gang Li, is that a smaller group than the large entourage he intends to bring with him can be formed to allow for more informal and thus more productive meetings to bring our negotiations to a mutually satisfactory conclusion.'

'The Chinese are past masters of polite and creative delaying tactics, should they want to employ them,' Laura felt bound to point out.

'Yes. That had occurred to me. It will be part of your role to ensure that the use of such tactics is kept under control. As for clothes—just bring a few basics. I've already ordered a suitable wardrobe for you, which will be waiting at our destination. I shall require you to be here tomorrow for eleven-thirty in the morning.'

Vasilii had turned his back on her to walk over to his desk before Laura could so much as acknowledge her understanding of the information he had just given her, never mind make her natural objections to his high-handed behaviour with regard to her working wardrobe, or tell him that she didn't like the way he had been so sure of her acceptance that he had already given instructions with regard to her clothes.

Only self-respect was one thing. Wilfully prejudicing the job she so badly needed if she was to be able to continue to help her aunt was another. Her aunt had sacrificed a great deal to bring her up. Sacrificing her pride now in order to help her was the least she could do.

It wasn't that the concept of an employer requiring a certain standard of dress was something new to her, or something to which she objected. She'd had a clothes allowance with her previous job. The thought of someone else actually choosing those clothes, though—especially when that someone else was Vasilii—sent prickles of a sensation she did not like trembling down her spine. Even worse than that—humiliatingly so, in fact—were the sudden unexpected and unwanted images which had produced themselves inside her head of delicate and very sensual silk and satin wisps of underwear.

Such images were highly inappropriate. The clothes that Vasilii had selected for her would be *work* clothes. It could only be because she had walked past a couple of exclusive lingerie shops on her way here this morning that those images had somehow lodged inside her head. No other reason. Vasilii Demidov might be the kind of man who had the style and the good taste to buy his lovers the kind of underwear that women loved, but she was most certainly not the kind of woman he would ever want as one of those lovers. Nor did she want to be.

'Here is the information you will need, and here is your contract.'

Vasilii had turned round, and now her face

started to burn. Get a grip, Laura warned herself as she took the papers he had put down on the coffee table within her reach but without touching her. Another unwanted stab of emotion pricked at her heart.

She knew his opinion of her. She knew he didn't like her or trust her. Everything about his manner towards her now that she had actually met him revealed him as a man who was corrosively antagonistic and nothing like the white knight she had fantasised about as a girl. So, given that, why should she feel hurt and rejected because he was making it plain that he didn't want any kind of physical contact with her?

It was safer to lose herself in speed-reading the contract than to allow herself to dwell on finding a truthful answer to that question, Laura acknowledged with relief as she read and then reread the contract.

As she had already known, the remuneration package was very generous, and with the added benefit of the bonus Vasilii had mentioned thrown in this six-month contract would give her the kind of financial security she needed. There would be a high price to pay for that financial security, though, Laura suspected. Not so much in the two hundred per cent dedication to her work which she knew Vasilii would demand, but in the cost to her pride and her self-respect in knowing that she was working for someone who disliked and despised her. Beggars could not be choosers, Laura reminded herself firmly. For her, right now, pride and self-respect were luxuries she could not afford. She needed this job.

Reaching into her bag, she removed the expensive pen that John had given her on the anniversary of her first year of working for him. He had had her name inscribed on it, and she treasured it as the gift of faith in her professional skills that she knew it to be. Dear John. Despite everything, he was a good man. He had been dreadfully upset about what had happened, though Laura suspected that a part of him had also been secretly rather flattered that his fiancée felt so possessive about him.

The contract signed, Laura replaced it on the coffee table and then gathered up all the other papers.

'You said you wanted me here for eleven-thirty tomorrow morning?' she double-checked.

'Yes. We'll be flying out by private jet. I'll discuss your grasp on the negotiations so far with you during the flight.'

There was nothing else to be said. Putting the papers into her bag, Laura headed for the door. She had a lot of very intense work ahead of her now, if she was to be able to answer any question Vasilii chose to throw at her tomorrow, but irrationally, as she walked back down Sloane Street towards the tube station, it wasn't concern about the work that filled her mind. Instead what was preoccupying her thoughts and her emotions was her own ridiculous and dangerous reaction to that heart-stopping moment back in the apartment when, unbelievably, it had seemed as though Vasilii was going to touch her.

The thrill of horrified revulsion she had felt then echoed through her again now. She went hot and then cold at the knowledge of just how foolishly and instinctively she had been on the point of going to him, reaching out to him herself, as though…as though she'd *wanted* him to hold her. Which of course she most certainly had not. She wasn't fourteen any more, and he certainly wasn't the white knight in shining armour she had imagined him to be in her girlish fantasies. He was autocratic, disdainful, sardonic and utterly without a single aspect of shining knighthood to his personality. But somehow her body had thrilled recklessly at the prospect of his touch. No wonder she had felt so horrified and revolted by her self-betrayal.

As she started down the steps to the tube station Laura couldn't help wishing that she hadn't had to accept his job offer. The reality was, though, that she hadn't had any other choice.

Once Laura had gone Vasilii gathered up the signed contract—her signature, he noted, was well formed and elegant, rather like Laura herself. That acknowledgement brought a swift cold frown to his eyes as he filed the contract. He had no wish to have any kind of personal thoughts about Laura Westcotte intruding into his private mental and emotional space.

As he straightened up from locking away the contract in his desk the group of silver-framed family photographs on the sideboard opposite caught his eye. The photographs had originally been placed there by his half-sister, when she had shared the apartment with him prior to her marriage.

He walked over to the sideboard and looked at them, reaching for the photograph that was almost tucked away behind the others—a photograph of his parents on their wedding day. His stepmother had given it to him on his eighteenth birthday, having gone to what he knew must have been an enormous amount of trouble to find it. After his mother's death Vasilii himself had burned all the photographs he could find of his mother, because he hadn't been able to endure seeing her image when he couldn't see her any more in the flesh. He had only been a child then, and of course—although he could never have admitted it to anyone—later he had regretted his emotional reaction.

His stepmother had guessed how he felt, though, although she had never said so. Her choice of that special gift to him had told him that. She had somehow known of the pain of his loss, and she had tried to offer him some comfort. Vasilii could still remember how torn his feelings had been when he had opened his gift—the sharpness of his sense of humiliation that his guard had been pierced by a woman's knowledge of what he believed to be a weakness he had successfully concealed from everyone but himself battling against the deep well of emotion looking at his mother's youthful features had brought him. Allowing oneself to need another person in one's life was dangerous. He had needed his mother but she had been taken from him. He'd had to learn to go on alone without her. That experience had taught him never to take the risk of loving anyone in a dependent way ever again.

Vasilii had never resented his father remarrying. He had grown up knowing that his parents' marriage had been in part a business marriage. That was the way things had been for the women of his mother's people. She had often told him that she had been proud to be chosen by his father. His father in turn had respected her and valued her. They had been happy together, and they had both loved him and shown him that love. That his mother's kidnapping and death had left his father devastated had been more than plain. If there had been other women in those years between her death and him falling in love with Alena's mother he had made sure that Vasilii had never known about them. He had been a man of strong principles and honour.

Vasilii had been pleased for him when he had met and married Alena's mother. Again, though, he had been caught off guard by the depth of brotherly love he had felt at the birth of their child, his half-sister. Of course he had tried to keep that emotion hidden—especially from Alena as she grew up. She had been so adept at winding their father round her little finger that Vasilii had been determined not to let her see that he was also putty in her small hands.

He had grieved for her and worried over her when his father and stepmother had lost their lives in an accident, and yet at the same time he had, he knew, built up a wall between them. For Alena's sake. It would have done her no good at all if she had seen him devastated, lost and made helpless, unable to protect her from her own loss. He had had to be strong for her. He had after all known the savage pain of that kind of loss. If he had been stern with her at times then it had been for her own sake, and now that she was happily married to the man she loved that wall had been justified. Because she had her own life now, with her husband and the children they would have together, and he was once again alone.

He had known from his own experience just how intense was the longing to cling to anything or anyone connected with the memory and the lost love of the one who had gone, so it had been for her own sake that he had encouraged Alena not to become emotionally dependent on him, whilst at the same time doing everything he could to protect her from further hurt.

It was because of the pain the loss of his mother had caused him that he had vowed never to allow himself to be so vulnerable again—not to a woman, not to any children that woman might give him, not to anyone. Some people might be driven to pursue love after such an experience, desperate to replace what they had lost, but he was not like that. The pain had been too intense, too much of an affront to his youthful male dignity. He had decided that he would rather not have love at all.

Unwillingly Vasilii was obliged to acknowledge that he and Laura Westcotte had something in common, in that she had lost her parents, too—and at a similar age to the age he had been when he had lost his mother. He at least had had his father. She, on the other hand, had had only an elderly aunt. If there was one saving grace within her make-up it was her financial support of her aunt. What? Did he actually want to find some good in her?

Vasilii put down his mother's photograph and turned back towards his desk. No, he did not. He thoroughly disapproved of and wanted to reject the way in which Laura Westcotte was managing to invade his private thoughts. Because whilst he knew that he had every logical reason to disapprove of and to reject Laura herself as well, he wasn't sure that he would be able to do so.

If that was true—and he was by no means prepared to admit that it was—then he must make sure that he found a way, Vasilii warned himself.

CHAPTER THREE

IT WAS time for her to leave for Vasilii's apartment. Quickly Laura checked her appearance in her bedroom mirror. After doing a brief check on Montenegro and its climate via the internet, she had decided to dress for the flight and their arrival there in a softly structured cap-sleeved tan silk jersey wrap dress that wouldn't crease, looked smart, but was not too businesslike, given that their destination was, from what Vasilii had told her, an upmarket exclusive resort. Pulling on a three-quarter-sleeved cream cotton jacket, Laura checked that she had put all the documentation Vasilii had given her to study in her laptop bag.

Just as she was about to reach for her trolley case, she stopped and turned round, going back to her wardrobe. The jewellery box was tucked away, right at the back of the wardrobe on the floor. It had been a gift to her mother from her father. He'd brought it back from Hong Kong for her. Traditionally decorated and lacquered, the box was in its own right a valuable antique, but its real value to Laura was and always had been the fact that not only had it belonged to her mother, but it had been given to her by her father. Their hands had touched it; they had exchanged loving smiles over the giving and the receiving of it.

The miniature cabinet was beautifully designed, with double doors that opened to reveal individual shelves, each designed to hold a different type of jewellery. The heavy, stylish, twisted gold earstuds that had been her mother's and which she had decided to wear in order to bolster her courage were on one of those shelves, but it wasn't that shelf she turned to first. Instead, her fingers trembling slightly, Laura searched for the special hidden catch that locked a small secret chamber in the base of the box. It was years since she had last unlocked it. She'd been a teenager who had hidden away inside it the photograph she had stolen of the darkly handsome man she had seen arriving at the school, behaving so protectively towards his young half-sister. That photograph wouldn't— couldn't—still be there.

Only when Laura finally eased out the small tray she saw at once that it was. Her hand shaking, she removed the photograph. Vasilii's features were instantly recognisable, even if it was a decade since she had snatched the photograph. Of course the only reason her heart could be giving that slow roll of breath-stealing shock was because she was angry with herself for not disposing of it long ago, Laura assured herself. Quickly she ripped the photograph in half, and was just about to throw it away when, on some impulse she couldn't understand, she found that instead she was tucking the two halves back into the secret space. As a warning to herself for the future, should she ever be tempted to put another man on a pedestal, Laura told herself as she replaced the drawer and then quickly removed her mother's gold earrings, closing up the jewellery box and restoring it to its resting place in her wardrobe before putting them on.

In his apartment Vasilii was just checking his watch at eleven-twenty-five when Laura rang the intercom. He certainly couldn't fault her timekeeping, Vasilii was forced to admit as he went towards the door and opened it.

'My driver is waiting downstairs for us,' he told her. 'He'll drive us to City Airport, and from there we'll be taken by helicopter to Luton, where we'll pick up a private jet. You have, I hope, familiarised yourself with the basic background to my negotiations?'

'Yes,' Laura confirmed as she walked alongside Vasilii heading for the lift.

Vasilii frowned as the silky fabric of the
dress Laura was wearing made a soft sound
as she walked. For some reason it made him
think of male hands against female skin. The
dress wasn't in any way provocative. In fact
it was undeniably plain and discreet, its wrap
style effectively revealing only the merest hint
of a V-neck and its hem neatly reaching Laura's
knees. However, the very fact that he had been
obliged to study her was enough to rearm his
hostility towards her. If he could remain completely untempted to give a second glance to
women who, in an attempt to attract his attention, wore far more provocative and insubstantial clothes than the dress Laura was wearing,
why was it that her dress managed to attract his
attention not just to its fabric but also—wholly
unacceptably—to what it revealed of Laura's
body? Her throat, her arms, the narrowness of
her waist, her legs and even the soft roundness
of her breasts. It was intolerable. And he would
not tolerate it.

Sunlight shone on the burnished sheen of her
hair and the warm gold of her earrings. Vasilii
made himself focus on their classical design,
but it seemed even they were determined to add
to his irritation and discomfort by nestling the

way they did on the delicate lobes of her ears, almost as though the weight of the studs might be too much for such fragile femininity.

They had only to walk across the pavement to reach his waiting car—it had taken a handful of seconds, that was all—but as his driver held open the door of the car for Laura, Vasilii was relieved to be able to walk away from the sight of her and around to the far door.

Immediately when he was inside the car he reached for his mobile phone and began to scroll through his messages, not by so much as a flicker of his gaze allowing it to stray in Laura's direction as they were driven to London's City Airport.

Laura didn't mind him ignoring her. In fact she was glad that he was. This morning by rights she ought to have been prepared for the impact of Vasilii's particularly corrosive brand of maleness on her system after the previous day, but for some reason the sight of him had brought to her far too vulnerable senses a fresh kick of unwanted sensual recognition of just how powerfully male he was. It didn't mean anything, of course. It was just that there were certain men—and Vasilii was one of them—who simply by virtue of existing forced women to be aware of them as men.

The transfer from luxurious limousine to equally top-of-the-market private helicopter was effected with all the speed and efficiency Laura had assumed it would be. She had travelled before with wealthy clients, and knew what to expect, so it certainly wasn't any lack of familiarity with a world in which she felt uncomfortable that was responsible for the nervousness she was feeling. She might want to deny it to herself, but she knew that the truth was it was Vasilii and Vasilii alone who was causing her to be so on edge.

In no time at all they were landing at Luton and being whisked efficiently to the waiting private jet. Laura had travelled in such jets before—some of them overpoweringly opulent and ostentatious. The interior of Vasilii's jet, though, was far more sternly practical and businesslike, and very much an office in the air—all black leather seating, chrome and glass furniture, and a fine dark charcoal-and-cream-striped carpet.

Vasilii himself didn't lose any time in getting down to work, either. Whilst there was an immaculately uniformed steward on hand to see to their needs, there was no offer of a glass of champagne, nor indeed any sign of conviviality, as Vasilii took his seat and promptly removed some papers from the case he had been carrying, immediately engrossing himself in them, having told the steward to bring him a cup of strong black coffee.

With his dark head bent over the papers on which he was concentrating, and with work of her own to do, she accepted the steward's offer of a coffee for herself. There was no reason or indeed any excuse for Laura to pause and let her gaze be drawn to Vasilii. In fact there was every reason for her not to do anything of the sort. But for some reason she just couldn't help herself. Hadn't it always been said that it was wise to know thine enemy? Laura attempted to defend her inability to look at something else. In a very powerful sense Vasilii *was* her enemy, in that she knew full well that he wouldn't hesitate to keep a check on her and to find fault with her if he could.

A brief telling glance from the paperwork in front of him to his watch, followed with an inhaled breath on her part at the powerful surge of the jet's engines as they took off, told Laura all she needed to know about Vasilii's control over every aspect of his life. She and her work would be subjected to exactly the same kind of scrutiny he gave every aspect of his business affairs, she warned herself, thanking the steward for the coffee he had brought her once the plane had levelled off. She certainly wasn't going to let the fact that Vasilii still hadn't really spoken to her affect her professionalism, Laura assured herself, and she opened her laptop bag to remove her own papers.

She'd checked the flight time to their destination—it was two and a half hours—and she would certainly rather have Vasilii ignoring her for as much of that time as possible rather than cross-questioning her about the information he had given her to read. Not that she had any qualms about her ability to do the work she had been hired to do. In fact she was rather looking forward to the challenge of what she suspected would be some very complex and challenging negotiations, with both sides bargaining hard for their own agendas and both sides determined to get what they wanted.

From his own seat Vasilii watched as Laura bent over the papers she had removed from her case. The way the light inside the cabin fell on her revealed the creamy slenderness of her throat, the heavy weight of the gold earrings once again drawing attention to the delicacy of her earlobes. Today she was wearing her hair held back off her face. A strand of it had escaped to curl against her neck, as though deliberately tempting him to reach out and wind it around his finger.

Somehow, out of nowhere, a feeling that was

totally unfamiliar to him and unwanted by him tightened Vasilii's stomach muscles. In denial of its raw betraying ache, he immediately stamped down on it and suppressed it.

The steward had slipped unobtrusively out of the cabin. Vasilii might not want to talk to her, but there were certain things she needed to discuss with him, Laura recognised as she skimmed through the notes she had made for herself the previous evening. In her previous job she had been used to acting on her own initiative—John had encouraged that. He had said that the only way she would grow was by making her own decisions and her own mistakes and learning from them.

She wondered if John and Nancy had managed to sort out their problems now that she, Laura, was out of the picture. He loved his fiancée, no doubt, and had been terrified of losing her. What must it be like to be loved like that, no matter what one did? Laura would never know. She simply wasn't the kind of woman who inspired that kind of love. John had often teased her that she frightened off the men who wanted to date her with her dedication to her career. She had to have that dedication, though. Money had been very tight after she had been orphaned, and she had learned young the importance of supporting herself financially.

A glance at Vasilii showed her that he had momentarily stopped working to drink his coffee, so getting up and going over to him, Laura asked, 'If you could spare me a couple of minutes? There are some things I need to check with you.'

Putting down his coffee cup, Vasilii indicated the empty seat closest to his own. Thankfully, as far as Laura was concerned, it was still distanced from it by a couple of feet. She wasn't ready yet to go too deeply into just what it was about the thought of any physical proximity to Vasilii that made her feel so tense and wary about her own possible vulnerability.

It made logical sense to reassure herself that it was *not* caused by his physical presence but by his interpretation of her morals and the curt warning he had given her. They had been more than enough to make any woman's pride sting, and to give her good reason to feel wary about inadvertently giving him the opportunity to misjudge her further. And yet niggling deep down in her conscience was a small seed of self-doubt that kept on reminding her of just how much she had once admired and desired him. But as a girl, and in a fantasy which had borne no reality to the kind of person he actually was. It was just her own determination to make sure that nothing she did or said gave Vasilii Demidov any opportunity whatsoever to accuse her of wanting any kind of relationship with him at all other than that of his temporary PA. Because she didn't.

Sitting primly in the seat, she began, 'The hotel where we'll be staying—'

'Is owned by a fellow Russian.' Vasilii stopped her, giving a dismissive shrug. 'It has been designed to attract the top end of the luxury market—Wei Wong Zhang mentioned it specifically. I have reserved two floors. The lower floor for Wei Wong Zhang's entourage and the top floor for Wei Wong Zhang and his family and for us. There are two suites—'

'The Royal Suite and the Empire Suite,' Laura acknowledged. 'I've studied the floor plans, and both suites have exactly the same floor space. I don't know if you've made any decision yet as to which suite should be allocated to Wei Wong Zhang, but if you haven't it occurs to me that to allocate the Empire Suite to him might be seen as a good diplomatic move.'

'Why do you say that?' Vasilii challenged her.

'Because of the name—the Empire Suite. Wei Wong Zhang is a student of the history of the Chinese Emperors and their dynasties.

It would be a subtle way of acknowledging his expertise in that field.'

Vasilii nodded his head.

'Very well. You'd better text ahead to the hotel and tell them. We'll be arriving several hours ahead of the Chinese anyway, to give us time to welcome them appropriately.'

'I thought perhaps a formal banquet, to which you could also invite the hotel owners? You did say that Wei Wong Zhang wishes to develop resorts in China?'

'Anything else?'

'Wei Wong Zhang's wife's name, as you know, is Wu Ying. Ying in Chinese can mean water flower. Bearing that in mind, I would like to order flowers for the suite that reflect that. It would be both a compliment to her and—'

'A subtle way of letting the Chinese know that we are aware of the nuances of Chinese negotiations?' Vasilii guessed.

'Yes. I went online yesterday after I left you, and did as much research as I could into the family and their likes and dislikes. Wei Wong Zhang is a sophisticated man with sophisticated tastes. He is highly educated and has travelled extensively in America, while Wu Ying has remained at home in China raising their daughter. If the gossip is true, Wei Wong Zhang has forced his wife to accept within their family circle his son by an American-Chinese mistress by giving Gang Li the status of "nephew". On the surface it seems, therefore, as though she has very little status within their relationship. Plus, Gang Li isn't just being groomed to take over the business, if what you've told me is true. He is also the existing power behind the throne of that business. However, Wu Ying is connected through her own family to some of the most powerful men in the Chinese government, so I would guess that Wu Ying is every bit as important to Wei Wong Zhang's business in her own way as Gang Li. If I am correct then it makes good sense to ensure that both she and her role are accorded proper respect. Of course if you have information that I do not have access to that contradicts that…'

'No, I don't.' Although Vasilii's tone was curt he was in actual fact extremely—if unwillingly—impressed by Laura's grasp of the situation, and her interpretation of it.

He was just about to point out to her that they had still to discuss her understanding of the negotiations so far when the plane jolted abruptly as it encountered turbulence in the atmosphere outside. The papers Laura had been balancing on her lap slid to the floor, but as she got up to retrieve them the force of the turbulence increased. The plane dropped so swiftly that she

lost her balance completely, the movement of
the plane throwing her in Vasilii's direction.

Instinctively, as she began to fall, Laura
reached out to steady herself, grabbing hold of
the first thing she could—only to realise too
late that, instead of clinging to some safely in-
animate object, what she was actually holding
on to was Vasilii's arm and thigh. Even worse,
the fierce jolt of the aircraft had thrown her
right across Vasilii's body, so that her face was
against his shoulder, her body resting against
his.

Arousal—male and urgent, fiercely demanding,
owning no master and recognising no control—
struck like lightning, burning away his self-
control, seizing Vasilii's body before he could
stop what was happening to him. The mindless
response of his flesh to the intimacy of Laura
Westcotte powered through him a hot desire
that seared and roiled like red-hot lava, with a
speed that overwhelmed his unwary self-control. Like border guards lolling in the sunshine,
his defences had let the intruder take control
before they could stop it.

He had somehow developed an extra set of
senses which now sprang up inside him, every
single one of them registering their awareness
of and reaction to the intimacy of her body next

to his. He had removed his suit jacket to work, and he could feel the warmth of her breath against his shoulder through the expensive sea island cotton of his shirt. He could feel her hair brushing his neck, and the impulse to lift his hands and slide them through its softness and then bind her to him whilst he punished the soft sweetness of her mouth for the way in which she had breached his defences to make him want her poured through him with molten heat.

The need he could feel beating within him was a savagely primitive male call to strip back the protective clothing of civilisation and modern manners, to rip through reality and go back to a place where instinct was all. Her presence in his arms, against his body, had destroyed the self-control he had thought so secure that he no longer even questioned the strength of that security, arousing within him a need and a hunger that filled him with shocked disbelief. Stunned immobility turned into an agonised inability to move as his own body subjected him to the fierce pulse of desire that heated his blood and his flesh, throbbing with betraying intensity only centimetres from where her hand was crushed against his thigh.

Sometimes in life things happened—life-changing events that came seemingly out of nowhere to wreak havoc and tear apart certainties. His mother's death had been one of those events, the accident that had killed his father another, and now there was this, Vasilii recognised as his mind and his body fought against one another for control of his senses. He wanted her, and he wanted her badly. Very badly. At some deep-seated, instinctive and totally male level he wanted her with a burning desire that right now felt like the rocket-fuel-raw heat of a volcano crushed down inside him, all too volatile and ready to explode.

This should not be happening. It must not be allowed to happen. He couldn't understand why it *was* happening. Not like this. Not with this overpowering intensity and certainly not with this particular woman. Neither his arms nor his flesh were strangers to what it felt like to touch a woman. He was a man, after all, even if the turbulent desires of his youth had been tamed to a more controlled recognition of the benefit of a discreet sexual relationship with a woman who understood his rules. It was true that the demands of his business empire meant that it was many months since his last relationship had ended, but he had not missed the woman who had been his lover. He had certainly not missed having sex to the extent that its absence could logically be held responsible for the intensity of the savage need that was possessing him now.

But it must be. Vasilii was not prepared to tolerate any other explanation for his reaction. His body had obviously decided that it needed a woman—but not *this* woman. In different circumstances the very fact that he had detected within himself any kind of weakness where someone he employed was concerned would have had him cancelling Laura's contract immediately and replacing her. However, as angrily reluctant as he was to admit it, she was far too necessary to the upcoming negotiations for him to do that.

She was in Vasilii's arms, lying across his body, breathing in the warm male scent of him in a way that made her both want to recoil from that intimacy and—even more dangerously— to move closer to it. Her face was still buried against Vasilii's shoulder. If she opened her mouth she would be able to feel his flesh and muscles, his collarbone through his shirt. She could feel the sinews of his arm beneath the fingers with which she was gripping it.

Most intimate and most shocking of all, though, was not the fact that her hand was splayed out against his thigh, sandwiched between their bodies as she lay against him, but that—wilfully, wrongly, recklessly and humiliatingly against all good sense and everything else she could think of—she could feel the demand of her own desire to seek *more* of that heat, *more* of that sensation of feeling the pulse of his blood, *more* of the knowledge relayed to her fingertips that beneath the expensive fabric of his suit trousers she could actually feel the silky softness of male body hair.

An explosion of female reaction shot through her, bringing her senses into shockingly sensual awareness not just of Vasilii as a man but of her own immediate instinctive and intense female response to that knowledge.

The raw, bare, unthinkable truth was that she wanted him.

At some level—against each and every one of the inbuilt warnings within her, against all logic and common sense—something in her hungered for him. That knowledge was like a white flash of burning awareness, searing her defences. It must be immediately banished, leaving only the pain of the scar on her conscience behind it.

Vasilii had laid down the rules of their relationship. She had accepted them. She had believed she would have no difficulty whatsoever in adhering to them. And yet now this accidental and unwanted physical contact with him had shown her that somewhere within her there was a vulnerability so dangerous that it rendered her fearful and doubting her self-control.

The plane had now steadied itself, and was flying calmly in a clear blue sky.

The turbulence might have come from outside the plane, but something told Laura that there would be no respite for her from the turbulence that Vasilii was able to create inside her.

How much time had passed? Seconds? A heartbeat? A brief interruption of real time that meant nothing and yet at the same time meant everything when he weighed it against what it had forced him to accept about himself, Vasilii acknowledged. He felt Laura shift her weight and push herself away from him in the thick, heavy silence that had now invaded the cabin. His senses—so dangerously sensitive to her now—could tell the difference between the scent of her skin, the warmth of her perfume, the fragrance of her soap. They urged him not to let her escape but instead to seek retribution for inflicting their torment on him. He wanted, he recognised on a brutal surge of self-knowledge, to strip her clothes from her body and his from his own and to wrap her in the scent of his own maleness until he had marked her as his own.

* * *

Laura could feel Vasilii thrusting away from her as she eased herself back onto her own feet. She couldn't bring herself to look at him. She dared not. If she did… If she did he might all too easily see in her expression, in her eyes, the shaming, shocking, humiliating reality that was her body's aching longing to go back to him.

How had it happened?

Laura didn't know. She'd never been the kind of person who wanted to do something simply because it was forbidden, so the fact that Vasilii had told her so coldly not to get any ideas about him was hardly likely to have been the cause. The loss of her parents had left her feeling unsafe, and with a need to protect herself from challenging circumstances. She'd grown up 'doing the right thing' and 'behaving responsibly' towards herself and towards others, which had made the accusations against her with regard to John all the more hard to bear.

Apart from that youthful crush she'd had on Vasilii there had never really been a time when she'd felt the power of her own sexual need as a force beyond her control. And even with that crush her desire had been youthful and innocent, not in any way as…as demanding as it had been just now. Was it possible somehow for something of what she had felt at fourteen to have sparked off what she had felt lying against

Vasilii's body? It seemed improbable, but what other explanation could there be?

Whatever had caused it, it must not happen again. Never. *Ever.*

Picking up her scattered papers, she registered Vasilii's continuing silence. His way of showing her his disapproval, she guessed. At least he couldn't accuse her of deliberately causing the turbulence that had taken her into such intimate contact with him.

Not causing the turbulence, no. But he *was* capable of accusing her of making use of it, Laura recognised. She was glad that she now had her back to him and he couldn't see the telltale colour heating her skin. The truth was that if he did choose to make that allegation she could neither entirely reject or deny it. From now on she must make sure that she kept the right kind of physical distance between them, and that everything she said and did where Vasilii was concerned was wholly and entirely professionally based.

Vasilii must never know how she had felt.

What had happened to him must never be allowed to happen again. Even if Laura had not been working for him, even if he had not had the doubts about her that he did, Vasilii knew that he could never allow himself to have a relationship with her. If he did he could end up wanting her too much, and letting that wanting get out of control. Just as he had wanted his mother to come back and not be dead. The pain of that had been like the burn of Russia's winter ice, when life returned to numbed flesh—searing, agonising, life-destroying.

Laura Westcotte must never know how he had felt.

CHAPTER FOUR

'VASILII, my old friend.'

Laura was glad of the opportunity afforded by the owner of the hotel's warm personal welcome to Vasilii as they stepped out of the helicopter that had brought them to the hotel from the airport to stay in the background—if only to give her the chance to take in in privacy the full, dizzyingly opulent splendour of the hotel itself.

Neither expense nor gilding had been spared in the decoration of the hotel's main foyer, Laura recognised as she surveyed an interior that seemed to be striving to combine European Renaissance and Rococo with Byzantine glamour via a nod in the direction of the vibrant colours of the East.

If anything could be scrolled, carved and gilded then it had been. If embroidered silks and sequinned satins could be used instead of simpler cottons then they had. The inner atrium to the foyer stretched up to what was surely an impossible height, with an indoor water display incorporating fountains and multicoloured lights that was truly mesmerising.

Columns inlaid with semi-precious stones and then gilded encircled an intricately worked mosaic floor, whilst the thinnest, most tanned, most designer-clad women she had ever seen in her life perched on ornate chaise longues. No wonder the poor things were wearing such brightly coloured outfits, Laura thought ruefully. They'd never have stood out against the sheer brilliance of the decor if they hadn't.

Despite the glitzy decor of the hotel, though, Laura couldn't fault the attentiveness of the smartly uniformed staff who had brought her hot towels for her hands and then proffered glasses of both champagne and fresh fruit juice for her to drink, whilst the owner of the hotel spoke proudly to Vasilii in Russian about the growing success of his newly opened hotel.

From what Laura had read its spa facilities were amongst the best in the world, catering as they did for both Western and Eastern tastes, whilst its restaurants and their menus had been created in conjunction with Michelin-starred chefs. With a world-ranking golf course and tennis academy as part of its complex, and the planned addition of an offshoot of a famous

Swiss cosmetic surgery clinic and holistic therapy area, the hotel was, Laura suspected, bound to be a success—even if her own tastes ran to something smaller and quieter.

The hotel owner was now telling Vasilii that he would show them up to the top floor and its suites himself, and as the two men moved away a very elegantly dressed woman of her own age glided over to Laura, walking so effortlessly in her very-high-heeled shoes that Laura immediately felt slightly envious. She preferred a lower, more comfortable heel to her shoes—especially when she was working.

'Welcome. I am Katinka, from the hotel's PR Department.' The other woman introduced herself in English. 'We have communicated already via e-mail?'

'Yes, of course,' Laura responded warmly. 'I am very grateful to you for your patience with regard to the last-minute request I put in for flowers for the suite our Chinese guests are to occupy.'

'They are here now—the flowers—and are being kept chilled in our florist's rooms. I have had some samples of what they plan to do made up for you to examine.' A small smile crossed the other woman's immaculately made-up face. 'I am very grateful to you for your suggestion that I study certain pieces of Ming Dynasty

Chinese art over the internet to get an idea of the kind of arrangements that are most appropriate. I hope you will approve of our interpretations of it. If you would like to come this way?'

Nodding her head, Laura walked with her escort towards the waiting bank of lifts. Katinka handed her a small leather wallet with some key cards in it.

'You will need these keys to access the lift to the top floor and the doors to its suites. I've had the maid unpack your clothes for you. They arrived yesterday. I envy you the clothes from the new season's ready-to-wear collections. Oh, I hope you don't mind my saying that?' she asked.

'No, of course not,' Laura assured her truthfully. She did not mind Katinka commenting on the contents of her new working wardrobe in the least. However, the fact that she was being supplied with such clothes certainly underlined the high status of her new role, and the demands both it and her employer would make on her. It was just as well that she knew Vasilii was the total opposite of sexually interested in her, otherwise she might have been anxiously worrying, after hearing that, that he might have a hidden agenda in mind.

Would she? Was that *really* what that spurt

of internal fireworks inside her body meant?
Or could it possibly mean instead that secretly
she liked the thought of Vasilii wanting to take
her to bed?

Of course not.

The men, still engrossed in their own conversation in Russian, were disappearing in the
direction of a sign that read 'Staff Only' whilst
Katinka ushered her into one of the lifts. Laura's eyes widened when she saw the mirrored,
crystal-embellished interior.

'This is a very glamorous hotel,' Katinka told
her proudly. 'It cost many, many millions of
dollars to build.'

'Wei Wong Zhang's entourage will have the
whole of the lower floor to themselves?' Laura
checked.

'Yes,' Katinka confirmed as the lift rose upwards. 'And we have made sure that one of the
private dining rooms on the banqueting floor
level will always be available for you. There
are, of course, separate private dining facilities on both floors, and in both top-floor suites.
Plus, we have made arrangements for a special welcome banquet to honour your Chinese
guests in our Michelin-starred restaurant tomorrow night, when they arrive. You will have
the best tables in the restaurant.'

'Those tables are in a central position within

the restaurant?' Laura asked. 'It would be considered an insult to our guests if it were to look as though they had been hidden away. Wealthy Chinese, unlike some of their Western counterparts, do not like to hide themselves away when they eat out.'

'As you requested, the tables will be set up in the middle of the room, with Wei Wong Zhang, his wife and nephew in elevated positions above the other diners, with their backs to the wall. We have, of course, Feng Shui'd the room as well.'

Laura's smile thanked the other woman, who then continued eagerly, her real feelings breaking through the professional mask of her role.

'This complex is a very exciting new venture for us here in Montenegro. All of us who are involved are so happy that we have this wonderful hotel to show to our visitors, and we are determined to make them feel so well looked after and pleased to be here that they will want to keep coming back.'

'I am sure that you will do that, Katinka,' Laura assured her. She liked the young woman, with the natural warmth allied to her professionalism, she decided, and was relieved to know that she would be working with someone with whom she felt it would be easy to get on.

The lift stopped, its doors opening onto a

good-sized rectangular hallway decorated in taupe and cream with touches of high-gloss black paintwork. The console tables and the mirrors over them were also lacquered a glossy black. The effect was an expensive look that successfully combined elements of Western and Eastern decor, Laura acknowledged, reflecting privately that she much preferred this to the lavish use of gilding she had seen earlier.

'These double doors ahead of us lead to the Empire Suite,' Katinka explained. 'This door here to our right leads to a corridor that links the Empire and Royal Suites. There are keys to it so that it can be kept locked. We have arranged for the lift for the Empire Suite to have a stop on it for the floor below, for the benefit of your guests.'

'Would it be possible for the Royal Suite lift to have the same facility?' Laura asked, quickly assessing the situation. She would have to check with Vasilii, but he might want to speak with members of Wei Wong Zhang's staff informally.

'Yes, that would be possible. Here in this drawer on this console table your guests will find maps of their suites and the rest of the hotel,' Katinka went on, opening the drawer to show Laura the glossily printed small concertina-shaped booklets, before closing it again to walk toward the double doors to the suite itself.

Half an hour later, when Katinka escorted her to the Royal Suite, Laura acknowledged to herself that both the accommodation provided by the Empire Suite and the hotel's organisation were superb and faultless. She had been delighted with the floral displays that had been made up, too—they were exactly what she had asked for, and Katinka had assured her that the fresh arrangements would be placed in the suite ahead of the arrival of the Chinese.

'I will leave you here to make your own exploration,' Katinka told Laura as she handed several sets of keys over to her with a smile.

Thanking her, Laura unlocked the connecting corridor door to the suite.

The Royal Suite mirrored the room layout of the Empire Suite, having three large double bedrooms, each with its own dressing room and bathroom, a study, a sitting room and a private dining room, plus two small bedrooms which Katinka had informed her were for the servants of those guests who preferred to have their staff on hand at all times.

As Katinka had shown her on the plan of the Empire Suite which room in the Royal Suite was to be hers, Laura located it straight away, relieved to discover that its decor was a subtle

blend of soft aqua, duck-egg-blue and off-white
that toned beautifully with the view of the sea
and the sky beyond the room's large windows.

It was a relief to have this breathing space
of time to herself, without having to worry
about Vasilii watching and judging her every
movement and every word, she admitted as
she walked into the dressing room. Her stomach muscles started to tense. She looked at the
wardrobe doors for several seconds, aware of
how ambivalent her feelings were about the fact
that beyond them lay the clothes that would be
her new working 'uniform'.

Laura wasn't naive enough to imagine that
Vasilii had had anything to do with the actual
choice of the clothes behind the closed doors.
He would simply have given an instruction, out-
sourcing that choice to someone else. So why,
then, did she still have this ripple of spine-tin-
gling 'something'—an emotional intensity that
had no right to be there—infecting what should
have been a simple swift and professional check
on something business-orientated? She was en-
suring that she had been provided with the right
kind of clothes to effectively manage her work,
that was all. Beyond these doors lay the necessary tools to equip her to perform her duties.
There was no reason, no logic and certainly
no need to have running through her head a

mental image of herself looking at the clothes that were hanging inside the wardrobe and then imagining the touch of Vasilii's hands on her skin. That was a totally illogical connection to make—and a very dangerous one. Because secretly she wanted to allow herself the indulgence of imagining how Vasilii's possession of her body would feel…

Alarmed—not just by the direction of her own dangerous thoughts but also by the effect they were having on her body—Laura yanked open the wardrobe doors and folded them back. The rail was filled with neatly hung clothes, whilst through the glass fronts of the floor-to-ceiling drawers she could see equally neatly folded things. The lower drawers contained dust covers over what Laura suspected were shoes and handbags.

A quick check through the clothes confirmed that they were all the correct size. But then Laura would not have expected anything else. As a working wardrobe it breathed style, simplicity and good taste. Laura was no fool. She could easily work out for herself that Vasilii must have given the instruction that his PA was to wear clothes that looked businesslike but at the same time would impress those she dealt with on his behalf, emphasising the status of the man who employed her.

She quickly decided that for this evening's formal dinner she would wear a well known and exclusive designer label's jade-green jersey dress. It had particularly appealed to her and she knew it would be perfect for such an occasion.

The drawers revealed a selection of pretty, feminine, but in no way cheaply 'sexy' underwear, each piece perfectly suited for the clothes that would go over it. Nothing had been left to chance. There would be no risk of damaging the impression that Vasilii wanted to give to the Chinese. All good business practice, Laura knew, and yet as she closed the wardrobe doors on the beautiful clothes hanging inside them for some reason an aching sense of loss and sadness filled her. Why? Would she really be feeling any better if she thought that Vasilii had bought her new clothes because he wanted her to parade in front of him like a dancing girl, commanded into his presence for his pleasure?

The clothes were a necessary part of her working life—of the image she must give to others in her role as Vasilii's PA. With that in mind she needed to be thinking about how best to project that image for the upcoming arrival of the Chinese right now, instead of thinking about Vasilii, Laura reminded herself. That meant looking at the clothes hanging in the wardrobe with that meeting in mind, and banishing those unprofessional thoughts that had so affected her senses. Vasilii's touch against her skin was not…

But she must not—should not be thinking like that. Even though only a very few hours ago she had been so close to him that… Stop that, Laura warned herself, taking a deep breath and deliberately forcing herself to think more professionally.

Whoever had chosen her wardrobe had known what they were doing, Laura acknowledged. Just as Vasilii had obviously known not only exactly the right size of clothes she would need, but also the type of styles that would suit her best in order to have instructed them. A man who could judge a woman's body shape and the style most suited to it so accurately was a rare male indeed. But of course Vasilii had not been selecting clothes for her as a lover. It had not been with a lover's gaze that he had visualised her body and then dressed and undressed it.

The shock of sensation that jolted through her had Laura stepping back from the wardrobe with her face burning as hotly as her body. What was the matter with her? Where had this wanton, reckless, almost delinquent urge to create the images that were causing such havoc to

her senses come from? Vasilii had known her
dress size because he would have acquired files
on her that revealed every single thing about
her prior to him offering her the job. That was
how modern business worked when it came to
high-status jobs and those who offered them.
The havoc her mind was trying to create was
pure folly, and something she needed to bring
to a halt—*now*.

The discreet dull buzz of her mobile phone
had her bending down to retrieve it from her
laptop bag.

Vasilii! Vasilii was ringing her.

'Where are you?' The sound of his voice—
wholly controlled, coolly chilly and sharply
acid—sent another zigzag of nerve-tingling
awareness zinging down her spine.

'I'm in the Royal Suite,' Laura told him.

'Good. I'm on my way up there. I'll meet you
outside the lift. I want to take a look at the Empire Suite ahead of the arrival of the Chinese.'

As he finished the call Laura was already on
her way to meet him. The freshly made floral
arrangements should be in the Empire Suite by
now, and checking it over with Vasilii would
give her the chance to make sure that they were
as good as the samples Katinka had shown her
earlier.

She was waiting when the lift doors opened,

glancing automatically into the lift itself and then freezing. Her heart lurched and her throat closed up with dread when she saw from her own reflection in the mirror at the back of the lift that she was wearing only one of her mother's earrings.

Not even Vasilii's frown and sharp, 'What's wrong?' as he witnessed her reaction had the power to bring back her mask of professionalism.

Her voice caught on her own emotions as she lifted her hand to her bare earlobe and responded, 'One of my earrings is missing.'

Vasilii glanced irritably in the direction of Laura's ear. The hand she had placed against it was trembling, and he could hear the shocked emotion in her voice.

'They belonged to my mother. When I wear them…' Laura shook her head, unable to continue, as misery at the thought of having lost something so precious overwhelmed her. Her mother's earrings meant so much to her. The thought that she had lost one of them was unbearable.

Vasilii could see how upset Laura was. He didn't need anyone to explain to him how much those precious things that had belonged to a loved and lost parent mattered, but neither did he want to be reminded of his own childhood vulnerability. Laura's loss and her emotional re-action to it was touching a place within himself that he didn't want to be touched. It made him curt with her as he asked, 'Can you remember when you last knew it was there?'

Laura tried to think back. She had renewed her lipstick in the privacy of the plane's wash-room, and she knew they had both been there then.

'On the plane—they were there…' she began to tell Vasilii, only to come to a self-conscious halt when, instead of relaying to her an image of her own reflection in the cloakroom mirror with both earrings in place, her mind gave her instead not only a visual memory of herself lying in Vasilii's arms but also a disturbingly sensual memory of just how it had felt to be there.

'On the plane…' Immediately Vasilii was physically reminded of those seconds—min-utes—when he had felt Laura's body touch his own, and the unwanted erotic effect that contact had had on him. Just the memory of it was pow-erful enough to have the same unwanted effect on him now, causing him to turn sharply away from her whilst he battled against the fierce ache in his groin and got himself back under control.

One word to Alexei and any number of willing women could be summoned to ease his every sexual need, Vasilii knew, but his own sense of pride would never allow him to take that route to easing his need. Vasilii preferred to battle against his own unwanted weaknesses rather than give in to them. And this inexplicable desire that Laura Westcotte seemed to arouse in him *was* a weakness.

The fierce, pounding urgency within his body had subsided to a raw ache. Half turning back to Laura, he commanded, 'Look at me.'

When she hesitated, he explained curtly, 'I'll take a photograph of the earring and e-mail it to the pilot of the plane so that he can get someone to search the cabin for it.'

Nodding her head, Laura tried not to feel self-conscious as Vasilii aimed his phone's camera, waiting until he had taken the picture before saying stiltedly, 'Thank you.'

Laura knew that the likelihood was that the earring had become detached from her ear during those few minutes of turbulence. She was genuinely grateful to Vasilii for what he was doing, but she also felt incredibly uncomfortable and self-conscious. It was a relief for her when he had finally sent the e-mail, with its attachment, and put his mobile away.

'Katinka told me that the private lift for the Empire Suite has been rejigged to stop at the floor where the rest of the Chinese delegation are staying. I wondered if you wanted me to have the same arrangement put in place for the lift for the Royal Suite, so you can also access their floor privately for informal meetings?'

'Yes, that could come in useful,' Vasilii agreed as they headed into the entrance hall of the Empire Suite.

Coming to an abrupt halt, he stared at the floral arrangements on the console tables either side of the hallway. Generally speaking Vasilii did not pay attention to floral arrangements. They were something that were just 'there'. But these were something else. Something about them not only commanded his visual attention, it also struck an unfamiliar chord within him that made him want to go on looking at them. Just as when he looked at Laura herself he wanted to go on looking at *her*. That was ridiculous. If he looked at her then it was because, given her history, he merely wanted to keep a check on her.

'Are these the arrangements that you designed and commissioned?' he asked Laura.

Laura swallowed hard. She had no way of telling from Vasilii's voice or manner what he thought of the flowers. Until he had spoken she had been feeling delighted with them. She still was, she decided. They were exactly what she had requested. Surely if she was to earn any respect from Vasilii as his PA then she had to prove to him that she was capable of making and then standing by her own judgements.

'Yes,' she told him.

The alarm ringing on Vasilii's phone had him reaching for it and telling her, 'We've got an hour before we're due to meet and greet the Chinese. Can you assure me that everything else in the suite is in order? Or do I need to check for myself?'

'It was in order when Katinka showed me round earlier, but as it will only take me half an hour to get changed I'd prefer to take another quick look now that I'm here—just to be on the safe side.'

A woman who put her duty to her work before her appearance? Very impressive. Except that she was probably saying that to impress him, Vasilii thought grimly, but he nodded his head and told her, 'I'll meet you at ten to six on the dot in the sitting room. Be there.'

And then he was gone, leaving her to make her tour of the suite as speedily as she could. As she had expected everything was just as it should be—even if she did now only have half an hour in which to get changed.

In the suite, and just on the point of stripping off his clothes in order to have a shower, Vasilii paused to check his phone. There was a message from the pilot of his private jet to say that a thorough search of the aircraft had not revealed the missing earring.

Vasilii put down the phone and started to unbutton his shirt—only to stop and retrieve his phone, thumbing through it until he found what he was looking for.

If his half-sister was surprised to be asked to commission on his behalf one of London's most exclusive jewellers to make an earring identical to the one in the photo he had sent her, and quickly, she knew him too well to say so.

Vasilii, though, as he continued to undress, wasn't entirely sure that he knew himself. He wasn't accustomed to acting on impulse—and certainly not for such a cause. It must be because Laura Westcotte had said that the earrings had belonged to her mother. Vasilii knew what it meant to lose a mother—and how it felt.

Half an hour later, hurriedly getting changed herself, Laura gave a small cry of delight and relief when her missing earring fell out of one of the folds at the neck of her dress, where it had obviously become lodged when it had fallen off. Quickly she put it safely away with its twin in the small jewellery box she used when she was away from home. Semi-superstitiously she felt reluctant to wear them again now, having only just found it, just in case somehow that prompted a second loss.

That was silly, she knew, but the earrings meant so much to her, and she had felt not just upset but also guilty at having lost one—as though somehow she hadn't taken enough care of them. Because she had feared she had lost it when all her attention had been on Vasilii and how he made her feel, and not on the fact that her earring had come loose. She had to stop thinking about Vasilii as a man and remember that he was her employer, Laura warned herself. She looked at her watch and then smoothed down the skirt of her suit. It was time for her to leave.

Vasilii was already in the suite's sitting room when she walked in, checking his own watch even though she was five minutes ahead of the time he had stipulated. She suspected that the suit he was wearing must have been hand-made to fit him so perfectly. Laura's heart did a small drumroll of something she suspected was sheer female pleasure at the sight of a man who looked so very, very male in every single way. Vasilii was one of those men who did not need to wear the kind of clothing that showed off his muscles for a woman to know instinctively that they were there beneath the smart tailoring of his suit.

And in addition to that she already knew they existed, didn't she? Thanks to that air turbulence. Laura could feel her hand curling into a self-betraying grip that mimicked the way she had clutched at Vasilii when she had fallen across him. It was amazing, really, how easily her memory could conjure up that moment—right down to the feel of the fabric of his shirt and beneath it the hard warmth of his flesh. Amazing? Or very dangerous?

Laura struggled to get her thoughts in order as Vasilii asked briskly, 'Ready?'

What was that scent she used? It was so delicate and light that it compelled a man to move closer so that he could analyse properly what it was. Laura Westcotte was a very clever woman. She obviously knew that its very delicacy would draw men closer to her, unlike those women who chose a much stronger scent which he personally often found repelled him and caused him to step back.

The outfit she was wearing fitted her perfectly—but then he wouldn't have expected anything else. Her measurements had been included in her dossier. Laura wore it elegantly as well, with a certain style that was her own. Her confidence, Vasilii recognised, was as subtle as her scent. And both could be dangerous to a man who became vulnerable to them. Possibly. But that man would never be him. A woman's moral behaviour—her trustworthiness, her reliability, the way she conducted herself, the way she lived her life—that was what he judged those in his employ on.

'It's time to leave.'

Vasilii's abrupt announcement had Laura nodding her head and turning towards the door. Her tummy was a seething mass of nervous tension, but she wasn't going to let either him or the Chinese know that. This was her first proper test as Vasilii's PA, and she was determined to see to it that she passed it with flying colours—even if those colours were begrudgingly given by the man who had made it clear that he would have preferred anyone but her to be his temporary assistant.

Several hours later, taking advantage of the pause between the final courses of the banquet they were being served, Laura did a quick visual check of the top table. Vasilii, of course, was sitting in the middle, in pole position, flanked by Wei Wong Zhang to his right, as guest of honour, and Laura herself seated on his left to act as his translator. Seated on the other side of Wei Wong was Gang Li, with

Alexei, the owner of the hotel, seated next to him, whilst Wu Ying was on Laura's other side, with the young woman who was her translator next to her.

Most of the other tables in the room were occupied by members of Wei Wong's entourage, with just a sprinkling of non-Chinese hotel guests to provide a discreetly curious audience.

The female members of that audience might be sparkling with diamond jewellery, but for Laura's money none of them could compete with the awesome magnificence of the jade necklace and earrings worn by Wu Ying. Laura didn't know enough about antique Chinese jewellery to be positive, but she suspected that they were genuine antiques and not copies. Even copies would have cost a fortune.

Laura had taken to Wu Ying the minute they had been introduced. One member of the Chinese party that Laura had not been able to take to, however, was Gang Li. Laura had been both initially surprised and then later on repelled by the way in which he looked at her and behaved towards her. She was used to fending off attempts at flirtation from men she met in the course of her work. Normally a certain degree of coolness and a lack of response was enough to get across the message that she wasn't interested. But what she had seen in Gang Li's speculative gaze had been more of a brutally sexual assessment of her body, as though it was a piece of meat. His gaze had remained on her breasts when they had been introduced, and it had remained there afterwards until thankfully she had been introduced to Wu Ying, thus enabling her to turn away from him.

Laura was grateful for the fact that she wasn't seated next to him—but that would only be a brief reprieve, she knew. As Vasilii's official interpreter she would be required and expected to liaise directly with the Chinese-American simply because he, too, spoke both languages and would be representing Wei Wong Zhang.

Even though Laura knew that Vasilii spoke and understood Mandarin, and she suspected that Wu Ying had a far better grasp of English than she was showing, she still meticulously translated for Vasilii whenever Wei Wong Zhang spoke.

The dinner was, of course, a very formal occasion, with several courses each accompanied by its own wine. Cautiously Laura only took a sip from each fresh glass. Allowing herself to become light-headed with alcohol would be a career mistake she was not prepared to make. That Vasilii was being equally abstemious, though, did make her wonder if he was being so because he had a naturally controlling nature, and wanted to keep his own eye on the game, or because he simply did not trust her.

Laura's translation of Wei Wong Zhang's conversation was exemplary, Vasilii had to acknowledge as he listened to her carefully translating a question Wei Wong had asked about Vasilii's desire to expand into China. She'd even managed to nuance her translation by speaking to him in Russian, so that even if he hadn't been able to follow Wei Wong's Chinese perfectly well he would have understood that Wei Wong might be slightly suspicious of his ultimate plans.

Tailoring his own response, he asked Laura to translate back, saying that stories he had learned of China's imperial greatness in past centuries had given him a lifelong interest in a country of so much potential and history, but that he was humbly aware of how much he still had to learn—which was why he was seeking a Chinese partner from whom he could do just that.

However, even whilst listening to Laura's translations, Vasilii was also keeping an eye on her manner towards Gang Li. So far she hadn't put a foot wrong, treating him with calm professionalism, but Vasilii had seen the way Gang Li had looked at Laura earlier. Such an open and obvious display of male lasciviousness was far from something he hadn't witnessed before. It happened all over the world, amongst every class and kind of man. However, when he saw it being exhibited Vasilii automatically and immediately downgraded his opinion of the man exhibiting it—whether it was welcomed by the woman on the receiving end of it or not. His father had always been respectful of women, whilst still being a man who was very much a man, and Vasilii had naturally modelled his own behaviour on that of his male parent.

Right now, though, it wasn't Gang Li's boorishness, nor Laura's calm, professional manner towards him that was demanding his mental attention so much as his own emotions: the anger and hostility he felt within himself for Gang Li. After all he had no reason to feel protective towards Laura Westcotte. Knowing what he did about her, it wouldn't entirely surprise him if she actually welcomed the other man's attentions. As mistress of a man with Gang Li's potential power—even if their relationship was short-lived—a woman like Laura Westcotte could improve her own career and financial prospects one hundredfold. She had slept with her mentor; it was merely a small step from that to sleeping with another powerful man who could advance her circumstances. If Gang Li's behaviour was anything to go by he would take her to bed tonight, given the opportunity.

The rush of fury that immediately seized him caught Vasilii unprepared. It was because there were issues here that could impact on his status if Laura slept with Gang Li that he was so concerned—and because as the older brother of a younger vulnerable sister he was automatically attuned to switch to 'protective mode'. It had nothing to do with Laura herself. Who she chose to have sex with or give her body to meant absolutely nothing whatsoever to him. All that concerned him right now was securing Wei Wong Zhang's goodwill with regard to his own planned investment in China.

It had been a long evening—a long day, in fact—but now it was finally over and the Chinese had retired for the night. Soon, thankfully, she would be able to go to bed herself, Laura thought tiredly as she followed Vasilii into their own suite. Whilst she felt sure that she must look as tired as she now felt, Vasilii wasn't exhibiting any signs of tiredness at all as he removed his jacket, dropping it down onto one of the chairs in the suite's sitting room.

'Wei Wong doesn't give much away, but I got the impression that he was impressed by tonight's dinner,' she told Vasilii as she fought her wayward and very unprofessional urge to keep on looking at him.

'Gang Li was certainly impressed by you,' Vasilii returned.

The comment—so unexpected—had Laura shuddering, openly betraying her revulsion at the mere thought of Gang Li before she could stop herself. She had hated the way he had looked at her—as though she was a…a lump of flesh, rather than a human being. Somehow he had made her feel even more than ordinarily aware of her sexual inexperience, and through it her vulnerability. She hadn't been able to help thinking that, had she been more experienced, she wouldn't have felt quite as threatened by Gang Li's unwanted attention as she had.

Even worse had been how, in the crush of formal thank-yous and goodnights when the party was ending, he had come up to her and—deliberately, Laura was sure—stood so close to her that his hand would have brushed the side of her breast if she hadn't moved away in time. She had felt so uncomfortable, so aware that her external apparent sophistication was not matched by the reality of what she was inside.

Professionally, all those years working with John as her mentor had protected her from the unwanted advances of men like Gang Li. Just as her teenage crush on Vasilii himself had been so intense that even after she had got over it no one else had ever been able to arouse her to such a fever pitch of longing. It didn't matter why she was still a virgin. And it had nothing whatsoever to do with Vasilii. It was simply a matter of circumstance—of not having met the right man at the right time.

Because somewhere deep inside her did a part of her still want to believe that Vasilii was that right man? *No!* Why was she allowing such disturbing and damaging thoughts to surface like this? A different sort of anxiety was beginning to fill her. She didn't want to think about either her virginity or her crush on Vasilii. She certainly didn't want to think about those far-off times when she had allowed her teenage imagination to furnish her with fantasies about being held in Vasilii's embrace and covered with passionate kisses, whilst he begged her to accept his love for her and told her that he couldn't contain his longing for her. Laura could feel her face burning just at the thought of her naivety and silliness.

Watching her, and taking in Laura's obvious distress, Vasilii demanded brusquely, 'I take it from that reaction that you don't welcome his interest in you?'

Why was he allowing himself to ask her that? Vasilii asked himself grimly. If he wasn't careful she was going to think that he was taking a personal interest in her, and of course he wasn't.

Determined to emphasise that, he added more curtly, 'I only ask because I don't want to have to deal with the kind of complications that are likely to arise if you encourage him. He is, after all, a married man.'

'I have no intention of encouraging him. Him or anyone else with whom I am involved professionally,' she announced, before adding emotionally when she saw his expression, 'Oh, I know what you think, but it isn't true. I *didn't* have an affair with John.'

'So you keep saying.'

'I'm saying it because it's the truth.'

Abruptly Laura fell silent. What was she doing? Why should it matter to her what he thought of her? It didn't—and it mustn't. And yet... Vasilii was moving about the room as she spoke, and for some reason the sight of the breadth of his shoulders tapering down to his waist had her focusing helplessly on him, the lean fitness of his body obliterating any thought of the unpleasant Gang Li.

With so much to think about from a professional point of view, there really was no excuse for the fact that—regrettably—it was the memory of Vasilii's body—lean, honed, his flesh warm to her touch as it had been when she had ended up in his lap on the plane—that Laura took to bed with her later that night. And it kept her awake for far too long, with her body aching and a fear inside her that once she did fall asleep she would end up dreaming of being with him in even more intimate situations that would increase that ache of female longing beyond all bearing.

CHAPTER FIVE

TODAY was the final day of what had been a tightly packed few days of negotiations, formal dinners and the only slightly more relaxing tours the Chinese had requested of the hotel, its environs and some of the coastline.

At least this morning she was going to be lucky enough to have one trip which would free her from the oppressive awareness that Vasilii was watching her every move and judging her ability accordingly, and from the even more unwanted visual attention she was getting from Gang Li. Wu Ying had asked if she could see a little more of the hinterland of the country, and if Vasilii could spare Laura to accompany her.

Now, after a working breakfast with the Chinese, Laura and Vasilii had returned to their suite to prepare for their individual programmes for the day.

'As you know,' Vasilii told Laura, 'Wu Ying has specifically asked for you to accompany her on this trip she wants to make today. Gang Li has volunteered to act as go-between and interpreter today, for what he has described to me as the less formal negotiations that will be conducted between Wei Wong and myself, without any other members of his retinue. I think I'm fairly safe in translating that as meaning this will be when the real business takes place.'

'I should really be there with you for that,' Laura told him, adding hastily when she saw the raised eyebrow he was giving her, 'Oh, I know you are perfectly capable of translating every nuance of what Wei Wong might say without Gang Li's help, but if I were to be there...'

'You could run some interference and give me time to think about what I'm being asked for in order to get the contract?' Vasilii guessed.

'I still have a gut feeling that it's Wu Ying who holds the key to a successful negotiation, Vasilii. Wei Wong will seek her approval because of her family connections. She hasn't said so much as a word to that effect. She's very discreet. But she has carefully dropped her cousin's government status and importance into the conversation often enough for me to know that they have a close relationship—they were brought up together by their shared grandmother. We shall be alone today, so maybe she will be more forthcoming. However, if you're having second thoughts about me going and you'd prefer me to stay, I can ask Katinka if she would stand in for me—she speaks some Chinese.'

'No. That won't be necessary.'

Was that because he didn't want the distraction of Laura's presence at his side? That was ridiculous. Why should her presence distract him? He had hired her, after all.

Nodding her head, Laura pushed her hair, which she was wearing loose today, behind one ear, preparatory to bending down to pick up her bag.

Vasilii, who was watching her, suddenly clicked his fingers and said, somewhat incomprehensibly, 'That reminds me. Stay here.' He disappeared in the direction of his own room, to return within seconds carrying a small cardboard box which he handed to her, saying, 'Your missing earring. Although it wasn't found on an initial search, my pilot e-mailed me yesterday to say that the cleaners had found it down the side of one of the chairs.'

Laura looked at him, her forehead creasing into a small confused frown, as she blurted out, 'That's not possible.' How could it be, after all, when both her earrings were tucked safely away in their box?

'I can assure you that it is,' Vasilii insisted crisply. 'Open the box and see for yourself.'

Surely that wasn't actually disappointment he was feeling at Laura's less than grateful response? What had he expected? That she would fling herself into his arms with cries of joy? That, once surrounded by the scent and touch of her, he would have every excuse to take advantage of the intimacy of an embrace she had instituted?

Almost reluctantly Laura opened the box. Sure enough there inside was one of her mother's earrings. She picked it up; its weight resting on her palm was familiar and exactly right. But it just wasn't possible that this was her earring. She knew that, and yet she was filled with an urgent need to rush into her bedroom to check that she hadn't somehow or other imagined that she had found the missing earring, and that instead of two earrings in the box there was only one.

She couldn't do that, though. Vasilii was standing in front of her, watching her, and if she wasn't careful he would start to realise and even question her confusion.

'Please thank the pilot for me.'

How stilted her voice sounded, her words more offered by rote than really coming from her heart. She took a deep breath and lifted her head so that she could look directly at Vasilii. Had his eyes really changed to a stormy warning grey, or was she simply imagining it?

'I really am grateful—very grateful. I was so upset at the thought of losing it.'

'Yes,' Vasilii acknowledged. 'I rather gathered that from your reaction when you discovered that you had.'

And had he done something to make sure that her earring was 'found' and returned to her because of that? Because he had been aware of her distress? Laura had another conundrum to battle with now. That sort of behaviour— that awareness of and compassion for the distress of someone else, especially someone else he disliked and would rather not have around him—seemed completely out of character for the Vasilii she thought she had come to know. And over what must to him have seemed such a trivial thing.

'I'd better go and put it away safely with the other earring.'

Vasilii nodded his head and watched her leave.

Why was it that the room suddenly seemed not just empty but actually physically a couple of degrees colder, deprived of some of its sunlight without her in it? Vasilii didn't like the feeling it gave him deep inside in that place where after his mother's death he had promised himself that he would never allow himself to feel pain again. He was relieved that Laura hadn't shown him the kind of exuberant physical delight in the return of her earring that his half-sister might have done, by throwing herself into his arms, because had she done so he would naturally have immediately put her from him in rejection.

In her bedroom, Laura held the small box containing her mother's earrings in her hand, her fingers trembling slightly. *What are you afraid of*? she asked herself. Not even Vasilii could have magicked away one of her mother's earrings without her knowing about it, and in any case, why on earth should he have wanted to? Quickly she opened the box—and released a gush of relieved breath. Both earrings were quite definitely there. Which meant... Which meant that she now had a third earring, nestling in its own box on the dressing table where she had placed it on walking into her room.

Reaching down, she opened that box as well, and placed the other one next to it. The earring Vasilii had given her was a perfect match, but it was not 'her' earring. Laura tried to think of all the possible reasons for a man to go to the trouble Vasilii must have gone to in order to get that earring made. She could only come up with two that made any kind of sense. The first was that Vasilii had hoped to please her because he wanted to take her to bed. She dismissed that immediately and unequivocally. If Vasilii had desired her—which she knew quite definitely he did not—he was the kind of person who would simply have said so, along with giving her a warning that all he wanted was sex and once he had tired of her their relationship would be at an end, Laura thought wryly. That left the only other logical explanation, which was that Vasilii had been so touched by her distress at losing her mother's earring that compassion for her had led to him having a new one made.

As though she was tasting unfamiliar food for the first time, Laura rolled the words 'Vasilii' and 'compassion' round her tongue together, all too aware of how mismatched they were—at least when it came to the prospect of Vasilii showing *her* compassion. But what other explanation could there be? She certainly couldn't think of one.

Very carefully Laura closed both boxes. By rights she ought to go straight to Vasilii now and give him back the earring, but she knew that she wasn't going to do so. Why not? Because he wouldn't take kindly to knowing that she had recognised his act of kindness? Did she want to protect him, then?

Yes.

No.

What she wanted to protect was their business relationship, which thankfully, for the moment at least, seemed to be working reasonably well. And she was enjoying what she was doing. It felt good to have been given such a challenging and demanding role. She felt it was stretching her and enabling her to really use her qualifications and her skills.

Before her short tenure as his temporary PA was over Laura was determined that she would win his respect for her professionalism and the quality of her work, no matter how grudgingly it might be given. And not just because that would aid her in moving up the career ladder when she got her next job. She wanted Vasilii's approval because... Because she wanted the satisfaction that came from receiving recognition for a job well done. Nothing more than that. Nothing at all. Letting Vasilii know she was aware of what she suspected he would see as an unwanted vulnerability within himself was not going to aid that ambition. So it wasn't because she felt anything personal for him that she wanted to protect him. No, of course not.

Of course not.

There was one small but important task Laura wanted to complete before she was due to meet with Wu Ying, and that was writing a letter to her aunt, who was someone who, having familiarised herself with modern technology, still preferred some of the more traditional forms of communication.

Laura smiled a little to herself as she sat down in the suite's sitting room with a notepad on her lap and a pen in her hand and began to write. And that was how Vasilii saw her when he walked into the room several seconds later. Her head bent over the notepad, an absorbed expression on her face. Laura was so lost in what she was doing that she wasn't even aware of his presence. Her lips moved as though she was speaking silently to herself, then she frowned slightly and caught up her bottom lip between her teeth, nibbling on it. She released her bottom lip, slightly swollen now. As though she'd been kissed? No. If *he* had kissed her then the whole of her mouth would reflect the intimacy of that kiss, and when he released it her lips would part and she would move closer to him, and then… A muscle jerked in Vasilii's jaw as he fought against the unwanted intimate sensuality of his own thoughts.

Laura was smiling now—a soft, tender smile, a smile of love—bending her head over the paper once again, and then tensing as she suddenly became aware that she wasn't alone.

Vasilii watched as the colour came and went in her face.

'I'm sorry,' she apologised, 'I didn't realise you were there. I was just writing my weekly letter to my aunt. She prefers letters to telephone calls or e-mails.'

'That must be time-consuming.'

'I don't mind. In fact I enjoy it.' Laura put down her pad and pen and told him truthfully, 'She was so kind to me when my parents died. I missed them dreadfully, and felt so alone, so lost, and in a way abandoned. She encouraged me then to write to them as though they were still alive, telling them how I felt. That helped me so much. It's so hard to cope with losing a parent—but then of course you will know that. Writing to them to tell them how I felt helped me so much. I owe my aunt such a lot that spending a little time every week writing to her is the least I can do.'

Vasilii felt his heart turn over inside his chest as he listened to her. With her words she had unwittingly touched on a place, a wound within himself, that he hated admitting existed—to himself, never mind allowing anyone else ever to know about it. No one was allowed to mention his mother to him, and yet here was this woman daring to do so—daring to speak of his childhood pain.

The need to protect himself sent a surge of anger racing through him. Turning on her, he demanded harshly, 'You say that, and yet when you could have helped her—when she asked for your help by chaperoning Alena in her absence—you refused to give it. You preferred to go to New York.'

'That was a misunderstanding.' Laura felt bound to defend herself.

'When my sister passes on to you a message from your aunt, asking you to stand in for her so that Alena is not in London completely alone, and you refuse, you call that a misunderstanding?'

No, what she called it was not receiving any kind of message from his sister to ignore in the first place, Laura thought grimly. But of course she couldn't tell him that without betraying Alena.

'Alena isn't exactly a child,' Laura pointed out.

'Not a child, no,' Vasilii was forced to acknowledge. 'But too trusting. And because of her nature and the situation of our family she was vulnerable.'

He meant because of his own wealth, Laura recognised, and of course what he was saying was quite true. Wasn't it only natural that as an older brother he would turn against a person he felt had refused to protect his sister, as he had turned against her? Especially after what had happened to his own mother?

'I'm sorry if you feel that I let you down.' What was she doing, apologising to him? She had nothing for which to apologise. But he didn't know that, and she couldn't tell him without betraying Alena. His half-sister might be married now, but, having seen at first hand the power that emanated from Vasilii, Laura could well understand that even the most loved and protected of sisters might not want to admit to not following his instructions.

It was a relief for Laura when Vasilii finally left the suite ahead of his own appointment. She tried her best to hold her own when she was with him, but that wasn't easy when all the time her own body was constantly reminding her of the desire it had once had for him. The desire it had *once* had? She was here for a purpose, Laura reminded herself—and that purpose was *not* to allow herself to dwell on the past.

Laura had apologised to him. Vasilii hadn't expected that. But then, as he was discovering, there was something about Laura that did have the capacity to challenge his judgements. She obviously cared a very great deal about her aunt. And her sense of responsibility where her work for him was concerned couldn't be faulted. Maybe he had been too harsh in his judgement of her? It was hard to know what was the truth about her.

The first thing that Wu Ying said to Laura when they met was, 'There is a change I wish to make to our tour. There is a winery I would like to visit. It is here.' She thrust a piece of paper with an address on it and a map under her nose. 'It is not far-off the way we were already to go.'

A quick check of the address and the map confirmed that Wu Ying was right.

'I'll inform our driver,' Laura assured her.

'We will go there first, I think,' Wu Ying continued firmly. 'My husband has begun to collect wine. I would like to buy some for him as a special gift from this winery.'

'In Europe we call them vineyards,' Laura explained.

Two uniformed members of the hotel staff sprang forward as they approached the main doors, opening them for their guests, and even though the doors were double width, with plenty of room for them to walk side by side, Laura automatically held back to allow Wu Ying to pass through first.

Today Laura was wearing a pair of beautifully cut white linen trousers and a softly styled tee shirt that matched the wedged heels of her espadrilles. She had a taupe knitted cover-up that went with the tee shirt folded carefully in a fabric bag with taupe leather trimmings that matched her sandals,

The immaculately polished limousine waiting outside for them had dark tinted windows, and its driver nodded his head when Laura showed him the map and asked in Russian—a language that most of the staff working at the hotel seemed to understand—for him to take them there.

Vasilii was meeting up with Gang Li at eleven o'clock, prior to a working lunch with Wei Wong Zhang at which Vasilii was pretty sure the latter's final decision would be made, if not passed on to him, as to whether or not Wei Wong was ready to go into business with him.

Although Laura remained convinced that Wei Wong's wife, because of her family's background in the government, had an equal if not more powerful influence on her husband's decision as the nephew who might be his illegitimate son, Vasilii had not as yet seen anything tangible to back up Laura's belief. Even if she was right, Gang Li was the official go-between, authorised by Wei Wong to act as his negotiator.

Vasilii suspected that behind the scenes a battle for who had the most influence on Wei Wong could be going on between Gang Li and Wu Ying. The brief text Laura had sent, telling him about Wu Ying's request to visit a vineyard and why, had in Vasilii's eyes proved that the battle had not as yet been won—hence her desire to find a special gift for Wei Wong.

Alexei had requested a meeting with him after lunch. The other Russian had already hinted that he would be interested in being involved in the development not just of a hotel complex with the Chinese, should Wei Wong decide to add one to his portfolio, but also in the development of less luxurious business hotels at the container ports. Reaching for his suit jacket, Vasilii picked up his smartphone.

The minute he walked into the sitting room of the suite he was aware of it—and so strongly that it stopped him dead in his tracks. Laura's scent. It hung softly and delicately on the air and should surely have been easily ignored. Sometimes he actually found himself having to move closer to her just to catch it, and yet here in this room today, in her absence, its chemistry reached out to him, enticed and lured him to pursue it, then surrounded and embraced him. How could something so ephemeral be so strong that it held him captive in a room in which he could neither see, touch or feel it? He was unwilling to step free of it—wanting… Wanting what? The woman to whom it belonged?

Angrily Vasilii pushed an irritable hand into his hair. This was a ridiculous nonsense that he had somehow allowed to slip under his guard. Because his guard was too weak where Laura was concerned? No, because it had never struck him that he would ever need to guard himself against something as unimportant as a woman's scent.

Unimportant? After the death of his mother he had spent hours just sitting in front of her open wardrobe doors so that he could breathe in her scent—that exotic blend of Eastern fragrances that had been so much a part of her—until his father had ordered that the wardrobe be emptied, telling him, 'I know how much you miss her, Vasilii, but she would not want this for you—that you should live in the past. It is time to let her go now, my son.'

His father had been right, of course. And now, remembering that part of his childhood, Vasilii was able to assure himself that the effect Laura's lingering scent was having on him was not because there was anything about Laura herself that could touch his emotions, but because of the connection between a recognisable scent and his mother.

Having explained that prospective and dangerous weakness away to himself satisfactorily, Vasilii headed for his meeting with Gang Li feeling freshly energised. However, just as he was about to step into the lift the doors opened to reveal Gang Li's assistant, who explained that he had been on his way to see him ahead of his meeting. If Vasilii could spare him a few minutes there was a certain delicate matter he wanted to discuss with him which might have an important bearing on the success of Vasilii's lunchtime talks with Wei Wong Zhang.

Nodding his head, Vasilii led the way back to the suite. He had a pretty good idea what the 'delicate matter' might be—a request for a bribe. Vasilii was no stranger to this kind of negotiation—he'd encountered such tactics in many different parts of the world. It wasn't something he liked or approved of. Nor had he ever asked for or accepted any kind of bribe himself. But this contract was large enough and important enough for him to recognise that in order to secure it he was going to have to play the game by the contract giver's rules.

In the sitting room of his suite he sat down, and then invited Gang Li's assistant to sit down himself. As the one with the higher status of the two of them it was important for him to show that status and take control.

Gang Li's assistant spoke quickly, as soon as Vasilii had indicated that he should do so, telling him, 'Gang Li is aware of the importance of this contract to your business. As you will know, his uncle relies on his good judgement and advice.'

'I have seen that Gang Li is very close to Wei Wong Zhang,' Vasilii replied diplomatically.

'Gang Li wants you to know that he feels you and he can work well together, should you be granted the contract. You are very ambitious for the success of your proposal—but then what is a man if he does not have such desires? Gang Li also has a desire of his own.'

Here it comes, Vasilii thought grimly. The only thing he really needed to know was exactly how much he was going to be asked for.

'And that desire is...?' he asked, continuing to play the game by its rules.

'Gang Li is very much taken with your assistant. Naturally as a married man, with a family and a reputation to maintain, he is not free either to approach or become involved with Miss Westcotte publicly. However, a word from you to advise her of Gang Li's...desire, and the importance he places on having that desire satisfied as speedily as possible, would be taken by him from you as a mark of good friendship, and it would significantly increase the chances of the successful completion of your negotiations with his uncle.'

Gang Li had sent his assistant here to tell him that Gang Li wanted him—Vasilii—to make Laura available to Gang Li for sex?

Fury, and a very male surge of something he didn't want to identify, surged through Vasilii. No. Never. No way. No way was any man going to be allowed to possess her. No other man. Ever. The thought of any man taking Laura to his bed filled him with such a possessive fury that he could barely contain it.

What?

The blind, automatic, gut-deep immediacy of his response shocked through him with lightning speed, burning away his defences. What was he thinking? What was he allowing himself to think? What was happening to him? Nothing. Nothing at all. His reaction was a momentary aberration, that was all. The very idea of him feeling possessive about any woman, never mind Laura Westcotte, was ridiculous, and something he would never allow to happen.

And yet even as he tried to deny it, oblivious to the nervousness of the man waiting for his response, Vasilii was forced to accept and battle with the reality of his reaction. It was because as his employee Laura was his responsibility, and that responsibility meant that he had to protect her, Vasilii told himself. Because Gang Li's suggestion was an insult to him as much as it was to Laura herself. He already knew how Laura felt about Gang Li. It had nothing to do with any desire for Laura on his own part. How could he desire her? He couldn't. To do so would be to break his own rules, and he never did that.

Inside his head Vasilii had a mental image of Laura's expression when she had let him see her revulsion for Gang Li. It was easier to focus on that than to analyse his own feelings. He had a duty to protect her from the other man's unwanted interest, he told himself, since in effect she was here under his protection. And right now, as far as he could see, there was only one way in which he could effectively do that and bring a halt to Gang Li's advances to her.

He looked at the waiting man and told him in an icy voice, 'That will not be possible.'

The assistant was frowning, and looking very anxious and concerned. 'Gang Li will be very unhappy about this.'

'As I would be myself if I were to give up my own mistress to him,' Vasilii told him coldly.

The look of dismayed shock on the other man's face said it all. He started to stumble over a halting apology as he backed away towards the door. Vasilii watched him in grim silence. He was simply playing a part he had chosen to play. It gave him no satisfaction to claim that Laura was his. After all she *wasn't* his—and nor did he want her to be.

CHAPTER SIX

IT HAD been an exhausting but an informative day, Laura thought tiredly as their limousine pulled up outside the hotel.

Wu Ying had turned out to be well informed about viticulture, and Laura had been surprised to be told by the other woman that she had recently set up a winery of her own in China.

'One day our wines will be sold all over the world, but for now we take small steps. The winery is my own investment—with the help of my cousin, who is my partner in the venture,' she'd told Laura on their way back to the hotel.

But it was what she had told her about the contract that Laura felt would be of more interest to Vasilii, and she was very grateful to Wu Ying for her unexpected frankness in discussing it with her.

'My husband places a great deal of faith in the judgement of his nephew,' she'd said. 'However, there are those who care a great deal for my husband's reputation and who do not share that faith.'

By that Laura took Wu Ying to mean that she did not share it. But then she had gone on to say, 'My cousin in particular feels that Wei Wong's judgement is being clouded by his… natural affection for someone who is close to him through the family bond they share.'

Here Wu Ying had paused, and Laura had wondered if that pause was a delicate way of hinting that that family bond was not so much one of uncle and nephew as father and son. But tactfully she hadn't pressed the matter.

Then Wu Ying had continued. 'My cousin does not believe that it would be to my husband's advantage or that of our country were Gang Li to be allowed or encouraged to take to himself too much involvement with the proposed contract with Vasilii Demidov.'

Wu Ying had then leaned over and, with an extraordinary gesture of intimacy for someone of her status to a foreigner, actually patted Laura's hand. She had smiled at her as she dropped what for Laura had been a total bombshell, announcing, 'I think that Vasilii Demidov holds you in high esteem, and when a woman holds the ear of a powerful man she can be wise for him in ways that his pride might not always allow him to be wise for himself in guiding him in the right direction.'

The car drew smoothly to a halt. 'I have enjoyed our day today, Laura,' Wu Ying said now, stepping out of the limousine and into the care of her waiting entourage, leaving Laura still sitting where she was, and still trying to take in the message she suspected Wu Ying had been trying to give her.

As she got out of the car and followed the other woman into the hotel, to be greeted by the uniformed staff opening the doors for her, Laura wondered how much of what she had been told was real hard fact and how much might be wishful thinking on Wu Ying's part. There was no doubt in Laura's mind that there was a very deep division between Wei Wong's wife and his 'nephew', and that a power struggle was going on between them.

She must, of course, report what Wu Ying had told her to Vasilii as soon as she could. As always the thought of seeing Vasilii and of being with him produced a rash of stubbornly female sensations that Laura knew had nothing to do with her work. She hated the way her senses were so vulnerable to his masculinity. It brought her far too close to the girl she had been—a girl who had coloured up in the secret darkness of her own bed because of the longing created by her own senses for a man who didn't even know she existed. It made her think and do things that were far more appropriate to that girl than the woman she ought to be. Foolish, idiotic things that only increased her existing vulnerability. Things like looking at Vasilii's hands and mouth whilst her throat went dry and her pulse raced, just as though her body was still aching for his kiss.

She walked into the sitting room of their suite, her heart thudding in such immediate betrayal when she saw him that she had to look away, just in case he saw that reaction in her eyes. Was this what happened to teenage dreams that were never fulfilled? Did they always come back to haunt you or was she just unlucky? Unlucky and foolish, Laura chided herself, and she reminded herself of her real role in Vasilii's life and tried to hide her real feelings with an outer air of professional confidence.

Vasilii hadn't had a good day. Unsurprisingly, Gang Li had cancelled their meeting, and then Wei Wong had cancelled their lunch—a sure sign, Vasilii suspected, that Gang Li was punishing him for denying him Laura. Looking at her now, as she stood in front of him, smiling confidently, her eyes sparkling and her general

air that of someone who had had a very enjoy-
able and successful day indeed, only increased
the angry confusion the way she made him feel
seemed to engender inside him.

'You'll never guess what Wu Ying has told
me—' Laura began, without any preamble.

'There's something I need to discuss with
you.' Vasilii cut across Laura's speech curtly.

She'd done something wrong. Laura knew
that immediately. And Vasilii's manner towards
her was so cold and harsh that it must be something very serious indeed. Her heart started to
thump uncomfortably heavily and fast. Whatever it was Vasilii wanted to say to her she
wasn't going to enjoy hearing it, Laura knew.

Instinctively wanting to divert his attention
she asked him quickly, 'How did your lunch
with Wei Wong go? Wu Ying says—'

'It didn't. Gang Li pulled out of our pre-lunch
meeting and then Wei Wong cancelled.'

Now the harshness in Vasilii's voice was even
stronger.

'Why?' Laura asked, even though her heart
was racing even faster. She could tell from
Vasilii's expression that somehow or other *she*
was to blame.

'Gang Li sent his assistant to see me this
morning, to pass on to me the terms under
which Gang Li was prepared to persuade his

uncle to agree to a contract. It seems that Wei Wong is inclined to favour us, but that he depends on Gang Li for directional advice and confirmation of his judgement.'

'Gang Li sent his assistant to ask for a bribe?' Laura asked. She could understand that Vasilii might not like that, but it wasn't exactly unheard of—and neither could she see how it could possibly involve her. Especially not in a way that could evoke the anger against her she could see so plainly in Vasilii's manner towards her.

'Yes.'

'How much money did he ask for?'

'It isn't money he wants,' Vasilii told her. 'It's you.'

Vasilii had heard the expression 'the blood drained out of her face' but this was the first time he had witnessed the visual impact of it for himself. Laura looked at him with huge shocked eyes, her expression filled with horrified disbelief and revulsion.

'Me? He wants me?' Laura wanted to deny what Vasilii had told her, to say that it couldn't possibly be true, but she could see from his expression that it was. 'No,' she told Vasilii in a shaky voice, her natural inner strength coming to her rescue as she gave a vehement shake of her head, and repeated unequivocally, *'No.'*

Vasilii hadn't said anything. He was simply watching her. Uncertainty and apprehension gripped her. Disorganised thoughts raced through her head. She might know Vasilii as a brother who was incredibly protective of his sister, but that did not mean that his male protection would ever be extended to include *her*. Quite the opposite, in fact, given his opinion of her. No man had ever protected her—not even John. Because she had never been important enough to a man, never had the kind of close relationship with one after the death of her father, not one would instinctively and automatically protect her. She knew that. She had grown up knowing it. She had even weathered the realisation that John wouldn't protect her. So why now, with Vasilii, did she feel such a sharp stab of pain? It was up to her to protect herself and she would do exactly that.

'I don't care what you've told Gang Li. I won't do it. You can sack me if—'

'You think I'd agree? That I'd allow anyone to abuse someone who is in my employ in any kind of way? Never mind suggest something like this?' Vasilii was furious. 'Do you dare to believe that I am the kind of employer—the kind of *man*—who could accede to such a loathsome request? Well, let me inform you that anyone who works for me in a business situation is my responsibility. I take that responsibility very seriously—just as I take equally seriously the behaviour of my employees in any way that it might reflect upon my business or on me. Naturally I told his messenger that what he was asking was out of the question.'

He *was* protecting her. He was angry with her, but he was protecting her. He was keeping her safe—just as she had longed for him to do all those years ago.

As he spoke Vasilii came towards her. Immediately Laura stepped back from him, afraid that her emotions would betray her. Her every instinct was to go to him and thank him, to cling to him and be held close to him. And of course she couldn't do that.

'There's no need for that kind of play-acting with me,' he told her acidly. 'That look of panic is more suited to a virgin fearing the possession of her first lover than an experienced woman in her twenties and it is wasted on me. After all, I know the truth about you.'

She realised that he had misinterpreted her reaction. Not that she was going to tell him that. She couldn't. Vasilii might think he knew the truth about her, but of course he didn't. In fact she was beginning to wonder if she even knew the truth about herself any more. She had come to work for Vasilii confident that he couldn't possibly affect her as a man, but increasingly he was proving to her that that was exactly what he was doing.

'In order to ensure that Gang Li knows there is no point in him trying to pursue you, and to bring an end to the matter, I told his messenger that you are in fact already under the protection of another man.'

Laura's heart skipped a beat. She had a very bad feeling about what was happening. A very bad feeling indeed. A bad feeling that came from far more than the revulsion that Gang Li's proposition caused her.

'What other man?' she asked Vasilii warily.

'Me,' he answered curtly.

'But it's not true,' Laura objected. Vasilii her protector? She his mistress? The two of them lovers? Oh, how foolish the female mind and heart were—allowing their owner to be taken from the brutal reality of being a piece of flesh to be traded for financial gain by men to whom she meant nothing to a place where she was a cherished, desired, longed-for woman loved so much by one man that he would do anything to protect her.

'Not for you or me. But for Gang Li it has to be seen to be true and accepted as true,' Vasilii warned her grimly.

'I'm your PA. If people start thinking that

I am also your mistress then my professional reputation will be called into question,' Laura protested.

'As it has already—via your relationship with your last boss,' Vasilii pointed out to her unkindly. 'It may not be a situation that either of us wants, but as far as I am concerned it is the best way of dealing diplomatically with things.'

Vasilii had had time to cool down from the heat of his earlier emotions, and he certainly wasn't going to tell Laura that his decision had been motivated by a desire to protect her. How could he when he didn't even want to acknowledge that himself?

Instead he continued, 'So tonight over dinner it might be as well if you were to act a little more as though you are my mistress—for Gang Li's benefit.'

He suggested that she should act as though she was his mistress—not both of them act as though they were lovers, Laura noted.

She didn't want to do it, but what alternative did she have? As Vasilii's recognised and acknowledged mistress she knew that she would be safe from Gang Li's unwanted attentions. Safe from Gang Li's attentions—but how safe would she be from her own desires? Desires which she was being forced to recognise were being fed by simply by being with Vasilii, never mind behaving as though they were lovers?

'Very well,' she agreed.

It was only later, when she was in her room preparing for the evening's final gala dinner, that Laura realised she hadn't briefed Vasilii fully on the conversation Wu Ying had had with her. She would tell him later over dinner, she decided. Right now she needed some time to herself, to come to terms with the new role she was going to be playing in public. That of Vasilii's mistress.

Her heart leapt inside the cage of her chest. Vasilii's mistress. And she a virgin who had no idea of what it took to please a man of Vasilii's sensual maturity. And if she *had* had that experience? What then?

The intimacy of the shudder of sensation that trembled through her locked the breath in her throat. This was too much. She shouldn't be feeling like this. It was a legacy of the past and had no place in her present. It was dangerous, humiliating and self-destructive, and it must be ignored.

The gala dinner intended to be the highlight of the negotiations, with a successful conclusion to the deal being celebrated even if the contract had not been officially signed, was now going to be more of an ordeal than a celebration, Vasilii recognised as he fixed the gold cufflinks that had originally been his father's into his dress shirt. Tonight was to be a formal dress event, and Alexei had assured him that their meal in the private dining room would have the full supervision of the hotel's head chef.

She really wasn't at all sure about this dress, Laura thought worriedly as she surveyed the back view of the beautiful gown that she had kept to one side for this special occasion without ever having examined it properly. If she had done so she would have discovered by now that, whilst the front of the column of silvery blue jersey had a high-slashed neckline, and whilst the dress's sleeves fully covered her arms, the back of the dress was completely cut away—right down almost to the base of her spine. Her bare flesh was covered with a sheer net fabric that made it look as though her back was completely bare. Added to that was the fact that the way the gown was cut meant that whilst it did not cling to her body it certainly moved with it.

Given what Vasilii had told her about Gang Li, wouldn't it be wiser to wear something rather less…well, rather less likely to catch the male gaze? However, a quick check of the wardrobe confirmed what she had already known: there was nothing else in it that would be suitable for this evening's event. There was nothing outwardly vulgar about the gown, it was true, but still Laura hesitated. Wasn't it the truth that this dress had been designed to be worn by a woman who was confident in her own sensuality, and even more confident about her ability to arouse the desire of the man for whom she was wearing it? A man like Vasilii, who would look at that woman and want her, who would touch her and hold her whilst she…

Shocked by the primitive intensity of the ache of longing that had come from nowhere to burn painfully low down in her body, Laura tried to distract herself by quickly sweeping up her hair into a soft knot—and then realised that with her hair up she would need to wear earrings. Her mother's earrings. And yet when she removed them from the box she found that she was hesitating and then selecting only one of the real pair, fixing the new earring Vasilii had given her in one ear.

They met in the suite's sitting room in mutual silence, mutually mistrustful and circling one another warily, Laura thought unhappily. But whilst her mind thought of Vasilii as her enemy her senses saw him in a very different light. She had known that in her room, getting ready, and that knowledge was reinforced for her now, as she felt the jerking tug of her own sensual response at the sight of Vasilii in his dinner suit the minute she saw him.

From the minute she had walked into his office she had fought against acknowledging what she was finally admitting to herself now, Laura recognised, and there was an ongoing draining battle constantly taking place within her between what she thought with her cerebral self and the way in which her senses reacted to him. She didn't want to be so intensely sensually aware of him, but the reality was that somehow she was.

Watching the way the fabric of Laura's gown moved as she walked made Vasilii frown against the effect the movement of her body was having on his own. Why—how—did she have the power to affect him in this way? It was perverse of his own flesh to be so susceptible to her, especially when he had seen women—even his own lovers—wear far more sexually explicit clothing and had remained completely unmoved sexually by that supposed allure.

'I see you're wearing your earrings.'

Why on earth had he said that? Vasilii wondered, irritated with himself. Why should he care whether she wore her earrings or not? He didn't.

'Yes,' Laura agreed, absently touching the one that had come from him and then dropping her hand immediately. It was totally illogical for her to feel that he might think she was touching the earring because it had come from him. After all, he didn't know that she knew that it had.

'We'd better go.'

Laura turned as she headed for the door, allowing Vasilii to see the back of her dress for the first time. The fierce stab of male desire that gripped him held him immobile in its savage hold, mauling him with its sharp, demanding bite.

Images that went totally against everything that he thought about himself as a man in control of himself and his sexuality were spilling through his mind in a swift dangerous flood. He could see himself kissing the nape of her neck and then her back, slowly, lingering over the scent and the taste of her, smoothing his hands down the naked curve of her spine, sliding them inside the soft fabric whilst he drew her against his body and cupped the unfettered weight of her breasts. He could see himself sliding the whole gown from her shoulders and letting it fall to the floor, to pool in a soft sigh of fabric that matched the exhaled breath she would give as he bent her forward and caressed her silken thighs, before sheathing himself in the moist, welcoming warmth of her sex. And she would hold him there as he drove them both to the exquisite pleasure of their shared release, before turning her to face him so that he could hold her in a final embrace whilst he kissed the sounds of her pleasure from her lips.

A fine sweat had broken out on his skin. He *never* had these kind of thoughts. They were irrational, unwanted, unnecessary—and damnably, unforgivably tormenting to a man who prided himself on his ability to control every aspect of the way he lived his life. On top of that Vasilii struggled to accept that they had been conjured up simply by the sight of Laura's naked back. How could that be possible? Anger filled him—against Laura, against the dress, against the impossible situation in which he currently found himself and most of all against himself. He should have listened to his initial doubts and not hired her in the first place.

And then Laura reached the doorway and he saw from the way the light was falling on her back that it was not naked after all, that a very fine film of fabric covered the flesh he could see through it. But it was too late. The damage had been done. Vasilii knew that he would spend many sleepless, tormented nights trying to deny the effect that the thought of touching her naked skin had had on him.

Five minutes later, in the reception foyer of the private dining room, busy with waiters circulating with trays of drinks, one of the other guests almost stepped back into Laura. Vasilii, who was walking behind her, automatically put out his hand to guide and guard her—and then withdrew it. Seeing his withdrawal in the mirror on the wall in front of her, Laura felt the pain of his rejection squeezing her heart. Vasilii might have told Gang Li that she was his mistress, but it was plain to Laura herself just how he felt about her. He couldn't even bear to touch her, he disliked her so much.

CHAPTER SEVEN

GANG LI! He had broken away from the group he was with almost as though he had sensed their presence as they entered the room, and now he was watching her, staring at her in a way that made Laura want to turn and run. She stopped walking, feeling vulnerable and very alone, but then Vasilii moved towards her, closing the gap between them without any hesitation, his hand initially beneath her elbow and then resting low down on her back. His touch was the touch of a man who was making it plain that the woman he was with was his woman. *His* woman. Vasilii's woman. The woman he desired and took to his bed to make completely and intimately his own.

Fiery darts of liquid heat shot through her veins. Unable to help herself, Laura turned and looked up at him, caught between the revulsion she felt for Gang Li and her inability to control her sensual reaction to Vasilii's touch.

A man could commit every folly there was for such a look from a woman. That was Vasilii's immediate reaction when he saw the look of helpless panic and plea that darkened Laura's eyes. A look like that from a woman like her could make a man feel that there were no lengths he would not go to in order to protect her from anything and everything that might hurt her. Instinctively the hand he had placed on her lower back curled round her hip to draw her even closer to his side—as though she was in reality his, as though they were in reality lovers.

He could feel her body trembling, and the soft unsteadiness of her breath against his throat. She would tremble like that in his bed, and her breath would be equally unsteady when he touched her—just as he would shudder with his own pleasure at their intimacy. No. That would never happen. Nor did he want it to happen, Vasilii assured himself.

Vasilii was simply underlining the fact that she was his mistress, that was all, Laura told herself. He had not drawn her close to him because he sensed her fear of Gang Li, and he had certainly not done it because he wanted her there. She knew that he didn't. So why was her body, why were her senses, reacting as though they had found a hero who was offering them the kind of sanctuary for which they had secretly longed and dreamed? It was beyond foolish—recklessly so—to let her body want that sanctuary so much that it was actually nestling into Vasilii, seeking and savouring his strength and his protection and that intimacy as though they were in fact lovers and it had every right to claim those things. And yet somehow she was powerless to seize hold of her own weakness and control it.

When had he last felt the warmth of a woman's body against his own like this? Needing him, wanting him, turning to him for something that only he could give her? Was he going crazy? Laura Westcotte didn't feel any of those things for him. She was simply acting out a part. He was a fool if he let himself think anything else. He didn't want to think anything else, Vasilii assured himself. But nevertheless he kept his hand and Laura exactly where they were as he guided Laura towards the dining room and Wu Ying.

Her own dress might be elegant, but there was no way it could compare with the gown worn by the other woman, Laura acknowledged. For this evening's formal dinner Wu Ying looked stunning, in a scarlet gown with intricate black bugle bead embroidery.

By the time they were halfway through the

dinner Laura also had to acknowledge that this evening Wu Ying, in direct contrast to both her husband and Gang Li, was far more animated than Laura had seen her before. Her conversation showed plainly her acute grasp of the complexities of the business deal Vasilii was presenting, and she spoke directly to him in her slow but excellent English.

Wei Wong seemed to be holding back, to be allowing his wife to ask more questions, whilst Gang Li did not seem to take much part in what was going on at all. He was drinking heavily, though—glass after glass of whisky— every now and again fixing a look on Laura that made her heart thump with discomfort and with something she didn't want to admit came close to a small tendril of fear.

The biggest surprise of the evening for Laura, though, came when Wu Ying leaned towards her whilst Wei Wong and Vasilii were talking to one another. 'I have learned of the offensive nature of Gang Li's behaviour with regard to you, Laura, and you may rest assured that it will not go unpunished,' she told her quietly. 'My husband has been very shocked and upset by the disclosures that have been reported to me by the aides to my cousin who have accompanied us here. He has agreed that my cousin is right to say that Gang Li must be relieved of his duties, and that for his own sake my husband must distance himself from him—despite their shared blood. From now on the negotiations will continue without Gang Li playing any part in them. My cousin intends to negotiate directly with Vasilii himself.'

She had been right to feel that Wu Ying had more power than they had initially been allowed to see, and it was a relief to know that Gang Li couldn't influence the outcome of the contract, Laura acknowledged, as Wu Ying changed the subject and began to talk about her winery and the plans she and her cousin had for it.

A lull in the conversation found her allowing herself to let her gaze drift towards Vasilii. He was still talking with Wei Wong, but as though he sensed her attention he turned to look at her, his gaze moving with deliberate intimacy from her eyes to her mouth to linger there. It was the act of a man visually staking his claim on the woman he wanted for his own. Sensual heat sheeted through her like an electric charge. Her heart was thudding wildly, her tongue-tip giving in to the temptation to moisten the sudden aching tension of her parted lips.

Beneath the table Vasilii tensed the muscles in his thigh against his body's physical reaction to Laura's response. He was playing a part—that was all. The desire for her his body was manifesting meant nothing in real terms. Nor would he allow it to do so.

The evening was finally over. Laura was relieved to see that Gang Li had already disappeared when she went to say her goodbyes to Wei Wong and Wu Ying.

Laura had decided to wait until they were back in their suite before passing on to Vasilii what Wu Ying had told her—however, they were just about to step into the lift when a member of Wei Wong's entourage approached and told Vasilii quickly that Wei Wong wanted to see him privately in his suite.

'You go up,' Vasilii told Laura.

Nodding her head, Laura left him to get into the lift. It was ridiculous, given the very reason she was here in this hotel with Vasilii, that all her emotions wanted to focus on was that aching pseudo-intimate moment when Vasilii had drawn her to him and she had felt so closely connected to and with him—as though…as though they shared a real and meaningful bond.

Laura closed her eyes against her own folly as the lift came to a halt.

The door to the suite opened to her pass key, the lights coming on as she went through to the sitting room. She couldn't go to bed. There might be things Vasilii wanted to discuss with her post his unscheduled meeting with Wei Wong, before the final official goodbyes in the morning.

Laura had just gone over to the unit that housed the minibar and coffee-making facilities when it happened: the sound of the internal door connecting the sitting room to the corridor opening, the rush of air its movement brought. Her immediate and instinctive movement was to turn towards those sounds—and then there was the nightmarish horror of seeing Gang Li coming towards her.

'No!' She denied him as she backed away from him but he ignored her, quickly overpowering her as he grabbed hold of her and pushed her back against the wall. Terrified, but determined to escape from him, Laura fought back, unable to stop herself from crying out when he forced both her wrists behind her back,

'You can call out as much as you want,' he told her brutally. 'No one's going to hear you, and no one's going to come. So why don't you make it easy for yourself and just give in?'

'Never,' Laura refused. 'Vasilii will be here in a minute—'

'No, he won't.' Gang Li cut her off. 'I've seen to that.'

He was holding both her wrists with one hand and the other was moving towards her breast.

Nausea clogged Laura's throat. She raised her knee towards his groin, and then gasped beneath the shock of the painful ferocity with which he jerked her back against the wall.

'You'll pay for that,' he warned her.

She could smell the fumes of his whisky-laden breath, and something else—something dark and dangerous, something that told her how much he wanted to degrade and punish her. He was reaching for her breast...

Angrily Vasilii got into the lift and punched the button for the suite. Wei Wong was obviously playing some kind of game with him, because he'd just seen him with his wife—who had announced that, far from Wei Wong wanting to talk with him, they were on their way to bed.

The whole trip out here had been an unmitigated disaster that had done nothing to advance his cause—quite the opposite. And now infuriatingly, given the problems that were facing him, all his normally obedient brain seemed to want to think about was those few seconds when he had held Laura close to him and for the first time in his adult life had known an immediate, instinctively irrefutable sense of closeness to another human being. It was because he had been caught off guard. He did not want to feel that kind of closeness. He did not need it. He did not like it. It was unnecessary, unimportant—unbearable because of what it had made him feel.

The lift sighed to a halt, releasing him from its captivity but not from the captivity of his unwanted and dangerous thoughts. Vasilii crossed the carpeted corridor and opened the suite door.

Desperate to free herself from Gang Li's bruising grip, Laura brought the heel of her stiletto shoe down hard on his foot—and then flinched as Gang Li raised his hand to hit her.

Vasilii realised what was happening the minute he opened the sitting room door. Without even having to think about what he should do he was at Laura's side, his arm protecting her from Gang Li's intended blow, his body protecting hers from the other man's lustful gaze. His fingers bit into Gang Li's shoulders as he tried to push him away from Laura, but instead of releasing her Gang Li pushed Laura forcefully to the floor before Vasilii could stop him, and then ran for the still open sitting room door. Vasilii wanted to go after him, to exact retribution but Laura had to be his first concern, and by the time he had helped her to her feet Gang Li had made his escape.

'Stay there,' he told her, after helping her to the sofa, and then stood in front of her so that she had no alternative but to do as he said whilst he reached for the hotel phone.

'I'll get a doctor for you,' he announced

Laura shook her head. 'No,' she refused, adding, 'There's really no need. I'm fine—just a bit bruised and shocked.'

'Why did you let him in?' Vasilii asked tersely.

'I didn't. He was already in here. He told me that you wouldn't be back in time to save me because of a message he'd sent you.' She winced as Vasilii swore comprehensively, and then apologised before reaching for the telephone again. 'I'm going to get Alexei to put a guard on Gang Li's room until he can be handed over to the proper authorities. He isn't going to get away with this,' he told her.

Laura nodded her head. She was still in shock from what had so nearly happened, but the last thing she wanted was for any other woman to be put at risk by a man who was quite plainly a danger to her sex.

She was distantly aware of Vasilii speaking to the other Russian, and the arrangements that were being made to ensure that Gang Li would be made to face up to the consequences of his actions, but her real attention was on Vasilii as he ended the call and came towards her.

This close he smelled of the aftershave he

wore—and something else that was hot and male and angry. Yet despite that anger she felt safe with him.

Vasilii looked at Laura. He had no doubt at all in his own mind that if he hadn't been stopped Gang Li would have raped her. Raped her. And he would have been partly to blame because he had not protected her properly. The feelings that thought set twisting savagely through him felt like the bite of a thousand lashes. If she had suffered because of him, because he had failed her...

Unfamiliar thoughts and feelings were struggling for life inside him. But it wasn't because of Laura herself that he was feeling like this. It was the principle of the matter, Vasilii insisted to himself.

She had started to tremble both inside and out, Laura recognised, her body held fast in the grip of reaction to the shock she had had. In fact she now felt worse in one way than she had done before Vasilii had rescued her—because now she had time to think about what could so easily have happened if Vasilii hadn't saved her.

Gratitude filled her, and her emotions spilled out into her voice. 'Thank you, for...for stopping him.'

She had said too much—been too personal,

Laura knew, and she watched Vasilii step back from her as though he wanted to reject her words and her with them. When had that tiny ache of pain she had felt the first time she had suffered his rejection developed the searing strength it had now? Laura didn't know. She felt drained and defenceless. The desire to beg Vasilii to hold her wasn't very far away, and it had to be resisted at all costs—because it wasn't real. It was simply a reaction—an over-reaction—to what she had been through. Better by far to put some distance between them than to stay here with him and that vulnerability.

'If you don't mind I think I'd like to go…to call it a night. We've got an early start in the morning,' she said as she struggled to regain some kind of normality.

Vasilii nodded his head as he stepped back from her, knowing that if he didn't—if he let himself stand too close to her—then he might… He might what?

Nothing. He swore inwardly to himself. Nothing.

CHAPTER EIGHT

UNABLE to sleep, her head pounding and her eyes gritty because she couldn't quite bring herself to close them, Laura looked at her watch. Half past two. She was perfectly safe. There was no need and no reason for her to lie here awake, she knew that, and yet at the same time...

She was longing for a glass of water, but she'd forgotten to remove a bottle from the minibar before coming to bed. *Stop thinking about it and go to sleep*, she told herself, but she couldn't. She was wide awake now, and so very thirsty. Thirsty—but afraid to get out of bed and go into the sitting room to get herself some water. Why? Gang Li wasn't going to be there, was he? She couldn't spend the rest of her life jumping at non-existent shadows because of one man. A man who had planned to rape her. A man whose unwanted touch against her skin had resulted in her standing beneath the pounding pulse of the shower before she had come to bed, wanting to scrub painfully at her skin.

The longer she lay there the more wide awake she felt and the drier her throat. Her longing for a drink of water was growing with every second, until in the end Laura could bear it no longer. She'd gone straight to bed after having her shower, pulling on the strappy top and shorts she wore to bed in the bathroom, and her longing for a drink of water took her straight to the sitting room instead of diverting first to her en suite bathroom to put on the robe hanging behind the door there.

With her hand on the sitting room door, Laura hesitated. It had been in the room beyond this door that she had experienced what might have been rape if Vasilii hadn't arrived to rescue her. And yet she knew as she hesitated that it wasn't just the fear that that experience had engendered that was keeping her here on this side on the door. She had another fear to face as well—a fear of the vulnerability that had made her want the intimacy of Vasilii's proximity. And not just because of the protection it had offered her. Why was she being subjected to, tormented by this growing, deeprooted and demanding ache of female need for Vasilii's touch? And not just his touch. Earlier, when she'd been comforted and protected by his physical closeness, wasn't it true that she had also recklessly craved an impossible emotional bond with him as well?

Angry at her inability to control her thoughts, Laura turned the handle of the door and stepped into the room beyond it. Intent on reaching the minibar and returning to her bedroom as speedily as she could, her mind turbulently preoccupied with her own too revealing thoughts, and in spite of the light provided by the almost full moon that was coming in through the uncurtained window, Laura still managed to stumble against the glass coffee table, sending the metal display piece resting on it sliding to the marble floor with a loud clatter. Quickly restoring the artefact to the table, thankful that no damage had been caused by her carelessness, Laura continued on her way to the minibar.

In his bedroom Vasilii lay motionless against the bed on which he had been lying, unable to sleep, trying to think of some way in which he could get over the problems that Gang Li's antagonism towards him was going to cause with the contract. In reality he was unable to think about anything or anyone other than Laura. The emotions that had gripped him when he had realised that Gang Li was attacking her still had the power to increase his heart-rate and fill him with a complex mixture of such intense emotions that he automatically wanted to restore his own personal default mode of denying he felt *anything*.

The best way to do that would be to go to sleep. But he couldn't get to sleep because he couldn't stop thinking about Laura. Not the contract, not any of the other things he should be thinking about, but Laura.

A sound from the sitting room broke into his thoughts and set off his own inner alarm system. Vasilii was on his feet and heading for the door the minute his brain registered the fact that there was someone in the other room.

With her back to the door as she opened the minibar, Laura sensed rather than heard the sitting room door open, her body registering the sudden movement of air caused by the opening door. Automatically and immediately her defence mechanism kicked in, fear streaming past her defences as she turned round to confront the intruder.

'Laura.'

'Vasilii.'

'I heard a noise.'

'I wanted some water.'

All Vasilii was wearing was a pair of thin cotton boxer shorts. The room might be in darkness, but thanks to the brilliance of the moon there wasn't very much of his almost naked body that was left to her imagination. And Laura recognised, as she fought hard to unlock her own body from its awestruck paralysis, that her imagination had in no way done full justice to the physical, living and breathing male reality of the six-feet-plus of solidly muscled manhood that was now standing in front of her.

Models and new men might wax, but the Vasiliis of this world quite obviously did not see the necessity to remove from their torsos that inescapably open, heart-thuddingly sexual message of masculinity that right now was riveting her gaze on the pathway it created down Vasilii's body, before disappearing beneath the waistband of the shorts that were riding low on the hard-angled bones of Vasilii's hips. Her heart was beating so heavily and loudly she could hear it herself, although it was several seconds before Laura recognised that she was holding her breath and needed to breathe. Just because she had seen Vasilii's naked torso? Not just his torso. She could see all of him, really—his torso, his arms, his legs, thighs that looked as though they had been hewn from solid muscle—apart from what was concealed by his shorts.

It was no wonder she was feeling dizzy—and that dizziness was not just caused by her inability to breathe properly, Laura knew, as she swayed light-headedly.

'Laura?'

Had he spoken her name out loud or merely felt the echo of mentally saying it crashing inside his chest? Vasilii didn't know. He only knew that the sight of her swaying on her feet had him crossing the floor to take hold of her, and that once he had... Once he had...

Vasilii was kissing her, and she was kissing him back, Laura recognised. She parted her lips eagerly beneath the sure, knowing intrusion of Vasilii's tongue-tip as it searched the sensitivity of her lips. Somehow he knew just how to use his power over her to turn her body into mindless delight and make her cling eagerly to him. His arms wrapped round her and she felt the full potency of his body impressing itself on her own. Felt it and wanted it. Wanted *him*, Laura admitted as her body responded to the intimacy of the feel of his flesh almost against her own, without any barriers between them.

It must be the shock of what had happened earlier—the shock of Vasilii coming into the sitting room when she hadn't been expecting him to do so—that was unleashing this soaring, crashing, demanding sensuality that was burning her up inside, Laura decided breathlessly, and her senses submitted to the demands Vasilii was making on them.

How had this happened? How could he be so aroused by one simple kiss? By the feel of this particular woman in his arms? It was beyond logic, Vasilii decided. Just as he, too, was beyond logic—beyond his own control, beyond anything and everything other than answering the need that was now driving through him.

Moonlight stroked Laura's skin in a pathway that led from her throat to her shoulder, its lure inviting his hands and then the kisses that followed them as she moved to his touch, her heartbeat making the pathway jump and tremble.

This was so much more than she had ever dared to imagine—too much more, Laura recognised as Vasilii's hands and mouth burned a platinum heat into her skin that sent her senses spiralling out of control and into a universe of previously undreamed-of sensuality.

Beneath Vasilii's touch, beneath his kisses, she had become another woman—a woman on fire with desire and need. Her body was not just responding to his touch but enticing and deliberately exciting it.

Looking down at Vasilii's dark head as he kissed her shoulder, she, too, could see the moonlight path he was following, and with a provocation she had not previously known she could manifest Laura found that she was moving her body, so that the path stroked down towards her breasts, shadowing the tumultuous desire of her peaking nipples. Another movement and the touch of her own hand, removed from its exploration of the hard-packed muscles of Vasilii's back, allowed her fingers to free her arm from the thin strap of her top, so that when she moved again it was her naked flaunting nipple that was caught by the silver pathway.

Distracted by the urgent rise and fall of Laura's breathing, Vasilii lifted his mouth from her shoulder and saw what the moonlight was now revealing. He was a man, with all the normal male desires; he had had lovers, enjoyed sex, but never had there been anything like this feeling storming through him now. It caught him up in its ferocity, flinging him headlong into its depths, searing him with its savage lash, possessing him with the same extreme intensity with which he knew he wanted to possess Laura herself. It knew no boundaries, no restrictions, no logic or law. It simply *was*, and he was bound to it—unable to free himself from it, he recognised. And he cupped her naked breast with his hand and bent his lips to the silvered torment that was possessing him.

Laura felt the growing crescendo of her own

driven longing, her need to clasp Vasilii's head so that he wouldn't stop doing what he was doing to her right now, with his lips and his tongue and his teeth, even as she could hardly bear the pleasure of it and half feared that it would destroy her. A sound—more than a gasp but thankfully not yet a scream—bubbled in her throat and spun into the shifting pattern of sound that was their mutually tormented breathing and the movement of their urgent bodies.

The moonlight showed the quicksilver of her bare flesh. It touched Vasilii's face as he bent over her, streaking slashes of powerful illumination on the sharp angle of his cheekbone before sending a shaft of pure steel over the muscles of his shoulder and back. How different their flesh was, and how different the moonlight's response to it—different and yet together a perfect match, a perfect whole. Laura surfaced briefly from the delirium of the pleasure Vasilii was giving her into a longing for the intimacy that would bring them together in that physical completion, only to be submerged once again in the new world to which Vasilii was taking her.

Never, ever before had he wanted a woman as intensely, as urgently, or as completely as he wanted Laura, Vasilii knew. Never, ever had the mere need to see a naked body aroused him so completely or filled him with the ferocity of desire he was feeling now. Never, ever before had the simple thought of seeing a woman naked driven him to such a place of agonised anticipatory need that the arousal that thought brought him was more intense than the full act of sex had been with anyone else.

'Vasilii…'

The sound of Vasilii's name, torn from her throat by her own desire as he slipped her top and shorts from her body, was as silvered with her desire for him as her body was silvered for his pleasure by the moonlight.

Vasilii's bedroom was a mirror image of her own, its bed wonderfully firm and wide before her as he laid her down on it. Her arms opened impatiently to him and for him as he pulled off his own shorts. The light coming in from the sitting room through the half-open door only told her what she had already worked out for herself, and that was that his body was beautifully and powerfully male, and that she ached to know and caress every intimate detail of it.

Laura's hands on his body, her breath against his skin, her lips tracing a line from his shoulder to his throat, had Vasilii sucking in his own breath and tightening his muscles, his stomach hollowing with the aching torment of his own longing. Logic, reason—everything he had told himself about never allowing himself to want like this were pale, insubstantial shadows of nothing that could not withstand the force of his need for her.

He kissed the soft curve of her belly and felt the anguished desire she was trying to control. He slid his hand beneath her knee and lifted her leg, so that he could kiss the smooth flesh on the inside of her thigh. She smelled and tasted of her own special warmth, her scent and taste inciting his desire to burn ever higher, even though he had thought that was not possible.

She wanted him. Oh, but she wanted him. And now even the hot sensuality of enclosing his sex within her touch was not enough to satisfy the ache of need raging inside her body. The intimacy of his touch and his kisses against her own flesh were driving her to a place where only sensation and need existed.

When Vasilii parted her thighs and leaned over her, his body cloaking her own in its hard male shadow, Laura welcomed the intimacy as eagerly as she wanted to welcome the intimacy of his possession. Her body, like her heart, was so ready for this, and for him. She could feel its waiting, pulsing softness. She could feel its tremor of knowing that a pleasure was to come that went beyond any uncertainty of the unknown.

One thrust—slow and purposeful. That of a man staking his claim on that which he knew to be his and which he couldn't live without claiming for himself. It carried him surely into the warm female embrace of Laura's body, and her muscles softened for him, then tightened around him to hold him.

One of them was trembling—shuddering with tiny involuntary movements of impatient longing—or was it both of them?

Vasilii started to thrust deeper and then stopped, his body and mind shocked by the awareness of a barrier that ripped a chasm between what had gone before that discovery and what he now knew. She was a virgin. How could she still be a virgin? The fact that she was stirred something deep within him that belonged centuries ago, to men who had prized and protected the sexual fidelity of their women—men who had known that the giving and the taking of virginity forged a bond that tied a couple together for life. Men who believed that the acceptance of such a gift committed them to the woman who gave it.

He could not make that commitment. He could not take such a gift from Laura. She had no right to offer it to him without first being sure that it would be valued as it deserved to be. A surge of anger and revulsion flooded him. Anger against Laura, for being what she was and in so being causing him such inner conflict. Revulsion against himself, for what had so nearly happened. What had happened to his earlier desire to protect her? Wasn't his behaviour every bit as bad in its way as Gang Li's had been? Wasn't he allowing his desire to dominate her and the situation just as Gang Li had planned to do? Wasn't he man enough, strong enough, resolute enough, to stop himself before it was too late?

For a handful of seconds Vasilii fought to control the urgency of his desire, and then he was withdrawing from her, moving back from her, reaching for his discarded shorts.

Laura couldn't believe what was happening. Just when she had thought that finally she would know Vasilii's possession he had withdrawn from her—and not just physically, she recognised as she watched him turn away from her to pull on his shorts. The outline of his body showed her quite plainly that, whatever the cause of his rejection of her, it wasn't anything to do with a lack of desire for her on his body's part.

Laura didn't know what to do or think. Her body was aching for what Vasilii had denied her with an intensity and a hunger that made her weak with need. She felt as though she was in the grip of a fever, half-delirious and fully distraught with the physical and emotional pain the shock of his abrupt withdrawal from her had caused, and she was unable to stop herself from adding to her own humiliation by begging him shakily, 'What is it ? Why…?'

Still half turned away from her, Vasilii answered, his voice grimly uncompromising. 'You're a virgin, that's why.'

He couldn't explain any more than that. He certainly couldn't tell her that somehow her vulnerability had undermined his defences, or about his own unwanted need to protect her. Because if he did… If he did then she would know that he was vulnerable, too, and he could never allow that. Instead he had to find another way, another reason.

Why was she still a virgin anyway? Vasilii had lost count of the number of women who had hoped to use his bed as a means of acquiring a wedding ring from him, and with it access to his wealth. Those women had hoped to use their sexual skills to persuade him. Laura had chosen the opposite route—that of offering him purity. It wouldn't work, though. He had no intention of making a commitment to any woman, and Laura, he told himself coldly, was no different.

CHAPTER NINE

HE HAD stopped, turned away from her, denied her because of her virginity? Laura opened her mouth to speak and then closed it again.

Vasilii could almost feel her confusion and her pain. He could certainly feel the ache of her continued physical longing because it echoed his own. If she were to touch him now…if he were to touch her… But he mustn't, and she mustn't—for her own sake. There was nothing for her with him. He had, after all, decided a long time ago not to allow himself to become emotionally involved with anyone, and she would want that. She would need it. He had to find a way to drive her away—to make her turn from him, to stop her from making him do what he must not.

Anger and pain burned with equal intensity inside him in a jumbled confusion of emotions that threatened to tear away the foundations of everything he believed about himself. They spilled out into the defensive cruelty with which he told her bitingly, 'I don't like traps. Especially when they are so obviously baited.'

Traps? He thought she was trying to trap him?

'I don't understand what you mean,' Laura protested.

'Oh, yes, you do. You're far too intelligent not to,' Vasilii corrected her. 'There's only one reason a woman of your age and in your circumstances—an attractive, desirable, intelligent woman—chooses to remain a virgin. And that has to be because she's decided her virginity is going to be a bargaining tool.'

'What? A bargaining tool for what?' Laura demanded. She felt both bewildered and shocked, her mind churning with emotion whilst her body was still awash with hormones and its desire for intimacy with the man whose words now said that they were opponents.

'For whatever she wants to bargain for—a rich lover…marriage… There are still men in this world who believe that only a woman's virginity can guarantee her worth and thus her value to him. I am not one of those men. In a lover I want and expect experience and skill. And, since I do not intend to marry, a virgin bride has no value for me. You made a big mistake in fixing your ambitions on me, Laura.

Even if I did want a wife, I'm not fool enough to be flattered by the gift of your virginity. The "See how special I think you are? I've saved my virginity for you and so you must repay me with the kind of commitment that comes with a wedding ring" scenario doesn't cut it with me. I don't intend to marry—ever. You've wasted your time—and not for the first time. What really happened with John? Were you hoping to persuade him to ditch his fiancée for you? The word is that ultimately he'll be the company's CEO and a very wealthy man. *He* was the one you were saving your virginity for, wasn't he, Laura?'

The tearing, slicing, stabbing agony saying those words caused him, and what that pain meant, drove him to fresh defensive anger. 'You hoped to tempt and torment him into a personal relationship with you that you could turn to your own advantage. How galling it must have been for you when he became engaged to someone else. No wonder his fiancée wanted rid of you—especially when she found out you'd made one last desperate attempt to win him over. And, having lost him, you obviously decided that I could take his place in your plans.'

He was deliberately whipping up his anger against her, Vasilii knew, as he drove himself to resist the aching longing that was still there

inside him. He couldn't give in now. If he did…
If he did then he would have opened the door
to a future that held the threat of a return to the
pain that had almost destroyed him once.

'No! *Never.* You have no right to say that.
And you are so wrong,' Laura insisted.

Vasilii's accusations would have been laugh-
able if they hadn't been so demeaning. How
could Vasilii even *think* those things about her,
never mind accuse her of them? The pain that
lashed into her cut her pride and her self-respect
to the bone.

'I have every right. And logically I can't be
wrong,' Vasilii contradicted her. 'For a woman
of your age in these modern times to still be a
virgin there has to be a reason—and none of
the ones I can think of apply to you, given the
enthusiasm with which you were ready to give
your prized and carefully guarded virginity to
me. No, Laura, you can deny it all you like. It
won't make any difference to me.'

Of all the scenarios she might have imagined
of being taken to bed by Vasilii, being rejected
by him because of her virginity was the least
likely of them. Ridiculously and humiliatingly,
she recognised, she had wanted him so much,
been aroused by him so much, that she had not
given her virginity a thought.

'Better luck with your next would-be target,'

Vasilii told her cruelly. He *had* to whip up his anger against himself and against her. It was the only way he had of stopping himself from taking her in his arms. The shock of that awareness stiffened every defensive instinct he had against what it meant, and made him fight all the harder to reject both Laura and what he was experiencing.

When she shook her head in rejection of his cruelty, and repeated with determined pride, 'You're wrong!' Vasilii made himself ignore the voice inside himself that urged him to believe her and to take her back in his arms.

It was unthinkable that he should give in to that need for her. He didn't even want to acknowledge it. Because if he did that would mean… That would mean that the straight highway of his life, free of the danger of emotion, had somehow taken a hidden turn that had appeared out of nowhere like a mirage in the desert. And a mirage was exactly what these… these ridiculous unwanted and dangerous feelings that were invading him were. A mirage that would disappear in the blink of an eye and as easily as love itself could disappear.

Pain from the volcano deep inside him that had never fully been sealed off burned hotly, spewing out the anger he needed to drive himself back to his empty highway. 'No?' he challenged Laura acerbically. 'Ask yourself, what kind of woman of your age is still a virgin? Only one who has some kind of hidden agenda.'

'Instead of saying that to me, you should be asking yourself what kind of man you are, Vasilii, and what it is that has made you so embittered and afraid to let anyone into your life,' Laura fought back valiantly.

Laura's words, coming so hard on the heels of the thoughts and feelings already tormenting him, were forcing Vasilii to acknowledge how different Laura was from any other woman he had known. She could touch places within him that no one else had ever come close to touching. She could arouse him emotionally as well as physically, to an intensity that no other woman had done. All the more reason not to get involved with her, the inner voice of his defensive system warned him. All the more reason to fight hard and deny the effect she was having on him, to turn his back on her, to turn away from her and reject her—even if doing so made him feel as though he was ripping a piece of his own flesh away from his body.

Silently Laura gathered up her discarded clothes and left the room. If those were tears she was holding back they were tears of female anger—tears of pity for all that Vasilii could have been and was not. They were certainly not tears for what she had been denied, she assured herself as she opened the door into her own bedroom.

Daylight, but the morning light brought her no escape from the humiliation and the despair of last night, Laura recognised as she showered and then dressed for the formal farewell meeting with the Chinese. She was a woman whose mind and body were fighting on opposite sides of a battle that neither of them could win. Her thoughts might be filled with and fuelled by the searing pain of her own angry awareness of Vasilii's unfair judgement of her, and her need to defend herself from the accusations he had made, but her body was refusing to listen to that anger or take into account her wounded pride. All it cared about was the persistent ache of longing it had been left with, thankfully dimmed now from its original raging intensity to something less likely to totally overthrow the tight self-control she was trying to keep over it.

It would make more sense and be far safer to whip up her justifiable anger against Vasilii than to focus on the ache inside her body, Laura knew. He was completely wrong about her reasons for still being a virgin. Remaining one had never been a choice she had made, it was simply something that had somehow happened.

Because for her there had only been Vasilii?

No! The Vasilii she had fallen for years ago didn't even exist. She had created him inside her own foolish imagination. The real man was nothing like the hero she had imagined. But Vasilii as he was had still aroused her. She had still wanted him. Was that because of the adrenaline of the terrible fear she had experienced contrasting with her relief at being rescued last night? Adrenaline was a very powerful hormone. Everyone knew that. And love was a very powerful emotion.

Love? She did not *love* Vasilii. She had far too much common sense to commit that kind of emotional suicide. Really? So where had her common sense been last night, then? That had been a mistake—a momentary failure of reason and self-control. It wouldn't happen again. What? Not even if Vasilii were to come to her now and start touching her? Start kissing her again as he had done last night?

The agonised moan produced by her protesting body had to be smothered in her throat. She had things to do—a life to get on with. In another half an hour she would be standing with Vasilii, bidding goodbye to the Chinese, and when she did she was not going to let him know so much as by a single breath just what she was now going through.

Morning, and not even the coldest of cold showers had the power to diminish the fiercely hungry ache of need still possessing his body. It seemed that nothing would—or at least nothing that he could do, Vasilii recognised grimly. What the hell was happening to him? Physical sexual desire was an appetite that he had always controlled within himself. It had never come close to controlling him—filling him, driving him, tormenting him so that he had hardly dared close his eyes last night in case he started imagining… Imagining what? That Laura was back in his arms? His senses surrounded and filled by the sight, the scent, the taste of her…?

Angrily Vasilii started to get dressed. By rights there should be nothing in his thoughts this morning other than finding a solution to the total disaster with this contract. By rights there should be no one on his mind other than Wei Wong Zhang. By rights…

Breakfast. Previously a shared private time of the day during which Vasilii had run through with her the working order of the day ahead and the targets he had set for it.

This day—this breakfast—they sat on either

side of the room service trolley in grim silence. In reality the last thing Laura felt like doing was so much as being in the same room as Vasilii, never mind eating, but she still had her pride—and that pride was demanding that she behave as though nothing out of the ordinary had happened at all. Professionally she still had a job to do, and she was determined to prove to herself that she could still do it.

Just how hard that was going to be had been brought home to her by the fact that somehow, despite the smell of freshly squeezed orange juice and piping hot coffee, her senses were still picking up and identifying the disturbingly male scent of Vasilii's skin. How was that possible? How had she become so sensually aware of him that she could recognise the intimacy of that scent? How? Did she really need to ask? She was sensually aware of him because last night he had left her body sexually unsatisfied, and right now it still hungered for him. She recognised his scent because she craved the intimacy of that scent on her own skin. Craved the intimacy of his touch, his kiss, his possession…

The hand holding her coffee cup trembled. Quickly Laura put the cup down.

Draining his own coffee cup, Vasilii reached for the copy of the *Financial Times* that had been delivered with their breakfast. Because he needed its protection to retreat behind? Protection? Why should he need protection? He would have needed some last night if things had continued to their natural conclusion. Laura probably wouldn't even have thought of that. Did she realise the risk she had almost taken? Did she realise how vulnerable she might have been had he chosen to take what she had been offering him? This morning she could quite easily not still be in possession of her virginity—all the bargaining power she might have been able to use on another man gone.

The bell to the suite buzzed, and the intercom crackled into life to announce the arrival of the hotel owner.

'It's Gang Li,' Alexei told them both without any preamble. 'He's gone.'

'Gone?'

Despite the icy coldness of Vasilii's voice there was no mistaking his fury. Laura found that she was flinching from it as it whipped round the silent air of the room.

'He was supposed to be under guard.'

'He was. But it seems that he managed to bribe the guards to let him go and give him an escort to the airport, where he hired a private jet. As he has dual nationality he could end up heading for either China or America.

I've spoken with the Chinese, and they're making arrangements to apprehend him if he tries to return to China. I'm sorry, Vasilii. Heaven knows how much he must have paid them. The guards have disappeared, of course, and we're only able to piece together what must have happened.'

Vasilii's grim nod of his head was his only response.

'I'm sorry,' he apologised to Laura, without looking at her. He concentrated instead on looking towards the wall once Alexei had gone.

'It isn't your fault,' Laura responded. Her main concern was for the other women Gang Li might target rather than herself. She, after all, had had Vasilii to save her.

It *was* his fault, though, Vasilii felt. He should have realised that Gang Li might try something like that.

'He isn't going to get away with this. I'll speak with Wei Wong,' he told Laura. 'I want to make sure that neither he nor what he did is allowed to disappear.'

Laura could see that he meant it. Why was it every time she told herself that she had seen something in him to destroy her teenage image of him as hero and protector he then did or said something that revealed the opposite? It was almost as though someone somewhere was determined to keep her... What? Hoping for the impossible? She would be a fool indeed to do that.

Laura had expected them to be the first to arrive in the room that had been put aside for their formal parting with the Chinese, but to her surprise Wu Ying was already there waiting for them—and on her own. As always she was immaculately and elegantly dressed—her smile for Laura was genuinely warm as she greeted her.

'My husband will be with us shortly,' she told them both, 'but there is something I must say to you first—about this terrible thing done to Laura by Gang Li. You may be sure that Gang Li will not be allowed to get away with what he has done. My cousin is determined on that.'

'I certainly hope that the justice he deserves is meted out to him,' Vasilii told her grimly.

'It will be,' she said firmly. 'You may be assured of that. And, with regard to the contract, my cousin has informed me that from now he wishes to be involved in the ongoing negotiations. Until now it has not been considered suitable for him to announce any government interest in this project. However, he is very impressed with your plans, Vasilii, and he has suggested that you and Laura return to China with us so that the negotiations can continue there.

'Laura has been a very strong and determined advocate on your behalf whenever we have spoken together. She has worked tirelessly and consistently to show me how mutually beneficial a business collaboration between us would be. Her honesty and trustworthiness have shown me that her respect and admiration for your business skills are genuine, and that has helped me to report back very favourably to my cousin.

'I have to confess that I was not entirely surprised to learn that the two of you are in a personal relationship with one another,' Wu Ying told them, adding with a pleased smile, 'For a woman these things are much plainer to see than they are to a man, and from the start I detected a closeness between you that was not merely professional.'

Laura couldn't bear to look at Vasilii. If she did she knew that he would see the pain and humiliation she couldn't hide. Not that her discomfort was Wu Ying's fault. She had brought it on herself.

He hadn't lost the contract—thanks in no small part to Laura. She had been right when she had warned him that Wu Ying might be more powerful than she seemed. Vasilii struggled with feelings as unexpected as they were confusing. Was that really a fierce sense of pride he felt in Laura for her professional skills? Was that an acknowledgement that her judgement in human terms had been better than his own? Was that also a primitive male need within him to publicly claim her as his own?

'I have my cousin's authority to invite you to join us at the winery of which he and I are joint owners,' Wu Ying continued. 'May I tell him that you will accept his invitation to return to China with us?'

'Yes, indeed. I shall be honoured to accept it,' Vasilii answered her, after a small but—for Laura—a telling pause. Vasilii knew that he really had no choice other than to accept. And it meant that he would have more time with Laura...

'Excellent. Then we shall celebrate the continuation of our negotiations instead of saying goodbye. Now I must leave you whilst I convey the good news of your acceptance of our invitation to my cousin and my husband. Our flight leaves at midday.'

Wu Ying had gone—a determined whirlwind of a woman who was now showing herself in her real light, Vasilii recognised, torn between relief at the good news about the continued negotiations and the realisation of just how much he might owe to Laura for that opportunity. She had seen what he had not, and in doing so she had shown just how very good at her job she was. And it wasn't just via her professional role in his life that he was being forced to recognise the influence she was having on him. Like the ever-shifting sands of the desert, vulnerable to the lightest of breezes, the foundations of his own rock-steady fixed decisions on how he wanted to live his life and why were being challenged and moved by her—even if she herself did not know it. And must not know it. He wasn't comfortable with what was happening to him. He didn't want it, and he certainly didn't like it.

'You didn't want to travel on to China, did you?' Laura asked Vasilii as soon as they were alone again.

He had betrayed that to her? Vasilii prided himself on never betraying any feelings he might have to anyone.

'If it's because of me and last night… If you're afraid…' She had to say it. Had to offer to let him travel to China alone—had to make sure he understood that his accusations against her were unfounded.

Did she think—could she possibly have sensed—that he feared his own inability to control the way he felt about her, his desire for her? Vasilii's pride burned.

'What is there for me to fear? You give yourself an importance you do not possess.' His heart was thudding in angry, defensive denial. Because both it and he knew that he had every reason to fear the feelings that Laura aroused in him. Because both it and he knew that somehow she had changed him, no matter how much he wanted to deny it.

Laura was too astonished by Vasilii's angry reaction to her question to respond. He had jumped to completely the wrong conclusion. What she had been about to say was that if he was afraid that she might do something silly he need not be. Instead for some reason he had assumed that she thought that *he* was afraid. Because of that he had immediately pushed her away with his harsh words.

Was that compassion she felt for him? If so, perhaps she needed to remind herself of his cruelty to her last night, and the harshness of his words right now.

He had protected her from Gang Li, she reminded herself. He had replaced her 'missing' earring. Which meant what? That she meant something special to him? She could hardly allow herself to think *that* after last night. And besides, why would she want to think it? She had to remember that the real Vasilii was the man who had told her last night what he really believed about her. The real Vasilii was the man who had turned his back on her and rejected her. The real Vasilii had made it more than plain that there was no role for her in his life other than the one she had already. The real Vasilii could never love her because he would never allow himself to love any woman.

Love her? Laura's heart crashed into her ribs with a force that momentarily deprived her of breath. What was she *thinking*? Nothing. She wasn't thinking anything—and nor was she going to.

He didn't want to dwell on Laura, but not doing so was proving impossible, Vasilii recognised. A woman who had worked as tirelessly behind the scenes as Laura had obviously done on his behalf had to possess a brand of loyalty that any man would value—especially in a relationship as close as their own needed to be. A *working* relationship as close as theirs needed to be, Vasilii underlined for himself. And that was the only kind of relationship they could ever have.

Laura was only doing what she had done for him because it was to her own benefit as an employee. There was nothing personal for him in what she had done. Everything that had happened should reinforce what he already believed about the danger of emotional relationships. It should confirm to him that he had been right to bring last night's intimacy to an end—even if his body was insisting still, via its unrelenting aching awareness of her, just how much it wished that he had taken last night to its natural conclusion.

Had he done so then this morning he would have woken up with Laura in his arms—in his bed. And right now that was where they would have returned to celebrate together this unexpected development that could still lead to success for his venture.

Was that what he really wanted? Laura in his arms and in his bed?

No. It was impossible for him to want that.

CHAPTER TEN

FROM the minute the plane had touched down in China's Shandong Province at just gone eight o'clock in the morning, after a twelve-hour overnight flight, with wonderfully comfortable beds in the Chinese jet, they had been treated as the most highly honoured guests as they travelled along the Yan-Peng Sightseeing Highway and into the Nanwang Grape Valley area.

Now, their destination was within view ahead of them in the hills, several miles outside the ancient town, surrounded by Ming Dynasty walls, and Laura thought that it would be impossible for anyone not to have their senses stirred by the beauty of this remote and very beautiful part of the country.

Wu Ying had already explained to them that China was planning to create its own wine-producing industry there. The winery owned by Wu Ying and her cousin, she had told them, had been modelled on French vineyards.

'And my cousin insisted that our house was to be more like a proper French château than a farmhouse,' she added, as their car started to climb up into the hills and they began to see the first of what turned out to be many acres of vines. 'We have already planted Cabernet Sauvignon and Merlot grapes. Next year we plan to introduce the Syrah and Viognier varieties,' she explained, before urging Laura to look out of the window so that she could catch her first glimpse of the 'château'.

It was truly magnificent, Laura admitted, and surrounded by a lake so that it looked almost as though the building, with its fairy-tale towers and gilded roofs, seemed to float on the water. When they got closer Laura realised that in addition to the lake the château was also surrounded by newly planted formal parterre gardens.

'My cousin and I argued about the design for this building,' Wu Ying told them both as the car swept up a long driveway before crossing a bridge over the lake and driving through a large gateway into the inner courtyard. 'I wanted something that was more traditionally Chinese, but he said that he wanted our home here to reflect the surroundings of the world's very best wines. It is his goal that one day we will produce such wines here.'

'It is all most impressive,' Vasilii complimented her.

And he was right, Laura acknowledged as they were bowed from the car by a smartly dressed major-domo and then escorted into a truly magnificent hallway, its decor very much in the style of the Palace of Versailles.

'I have arranged a tour for you tomorrow—not just of our vineyard but also of the coastal Treaty Ports, built here originally by the British for foreign trade during the Opium Wars. We get many English tourists wanting to visit, and my cousin believes that this will one day be a good place to build a hotel complex such as the one in Montenegro. For now, though, Chan will show you to your room. We have given you our most special tower bedroom. It is very romantic,' she told them with a pleased smile. 'It has worked out well that you are able to share a room, as my cousin complains that we do not have enough bedrooms here to accommodate his entourage.'

Laura had already opened her mouth to explain that they would prefer *not* to share a room, but Vasilii was shaking his head and frowning at her and Laura knew why. If they were to say now that they were not lovers, then Wu Ying would be embarrassed—especially as she had already said that she had thought there was a

romantic connection between them even before
Vasilii had lied to Gang Li and told him that
they were lovers.

However, whilst Laura knew why Vasilii had
given her that silent warning to remain silent
and say nothing, she also knew that she could
not possibly share a room with him. Right now,
though, she had no choice other than to follow
Vasilii as Chan, the major-domo, led the way
not to a fairy-tale sweeping staircase but instead
to a lift that was cleverly disguised as one of
several marble columns.

The lift took them straight up to a circular
upper hallway, with magnificent views of the
countryside and the vines beyond the château
through its windows. Several corridors radi-
ated off the hallway. The one they were shown
down had small windowed cabinets built into
the walls which held beautiful pieces of Chinese art. Laura would have liked to have been
able to look more closely at them, but Chan was
obviously keen to show them straight to their
room.

Their room. Laura's heart did a high dive that
left her head spinning.

The corridor came to an end outside a pair of
ornately decorated doors, which Chan opened
with a flourish.

The first thing Laura saw when Vasilii

stepped back so that she could precede him inside was the shaft of sunlight coming in from the high narrow window opposite the door. Beyond it she could see the distant mountains, with their peaks wreathed in mist. Or was she simply focusing on the view beyond the room because she was afraid to look at the room itself? But of course she had to do so, and—just as she had dreaded—it was dominated by a huge bed, with a Louis XV–style carved bedhead. A *huge* bed. Not even two singles that had been pushed together. A huge bed and two stately but uncomfortable-looking chairs which were drawn up either side of the marble fireplace. Not even a sofa, then.

'We can't both sleep here,' she told Vasilii as soon as Chan had gone, leaving them alone together in the room.

'We have to,' Vasilii told her grimly. 'It's not what either of us would have chosen, but it's hardly the end of the world. We're only here for a handful of days, after all, and I am not prepared to prejudice or risk a successful conclusion to my discussions at this stage.'

'We aren't just going to have to share a room, we're going to have to share a bed as well,' Laura stressed.

'A very large bed. And since I would have thought I have already demonstrated to you that

I am perfectly capable of not touching you, and you have insisted to me that you shared a suite with your previous boss without—'

'A suite. Not a bedroom.'

'You were found in his bed.'

'But he hadn't slept in it.'

'You're turning an admittedly unwanted situation into a dramatic production that it doesn't warrant. All we need to do is agree that neither of us wants to have any kind of sexual or intimate contact with the other and that can be an end to the matter. On the other hand there is always a chair. Not that they look particularly comfortable. Now, what time did Wu Ying say her cousin would be arriving?'

'At four o'clock this afternoon.'

'That gives us two hours. I want to go over some of my costings before the meeting, but first I want a shower. I expect you feel the same. Do you want to use the bathroom first?'

Laura nodded her head. What else could she do? Vasilii was obviously taking it for granted that they were going to share this room, and its bed, and she could hardly object after what he had said without risking having him ask her exactly why she was objecting. And she couldn't give him the answer to that question, could she? Not when it would mean admitting to him that she was afraid of the way being so close to him made her feel.

And what was that?

Laura felt a shudder of sensation and longing run right through her, from the top of her head right down into her toes. In fact it was so intense that it made her curl those toes up inside her shoes. Being close to Vasilii would make her feel just like that. Lying close to him in bed would intensify it a thousandfold. But her pride wouldn't allow her to tell him that she couldn't share that bed because she was afraid of her own longing for him. What woman's would?

It had been a long day, culminating in a discussion over dinner between Vasilii and Wu Ying's cousin from the government which had resulted in the formal offer of a contract.

Now, tired but buoyed up with the feeling of euphoria that came from being part of such a successful conclusion, Laura was actually able to put aside her anxiety about sharing a bed with Vasilii as he unlocked the door to their room.

'An excellent result,' Vasilii told her once they were inside. 'The terms we're being offered are better than I'd hoped for.'

It was ridiculous for her to feel a surge of pleasure and belonging just because he had used the word 'we', Laura warned herself, discreetly touching her earlobes to make sure that her earrings were still in place.

She realised that she had not been discreet enough when she saw that Vasilii was watching her.

'I'm almost afraid to wear them after so nearly losing one,' she felt obliged to admit.

'So why did you?' Vasilii asked her.

It was not just totally irrational but actively dangerous as well, this need he felt to keep her here with him, to talk to her properly without any barriers between them.

'I always wear them when I feel I need some extra-special help or good luck. It's silly, I know, but because they were my mother's wearing them makes me feel as though a part of her is with me.'

Why had she told him that? He would think she was totally idiotic.

'Why did you feel you needed some good luck?'

Why had she started this? Now she was going to look a total fool. 'I wanted it for the contract,' she admitted reluctantly.

Vasilii had turned away from her to walk over to the window. Now he turned round and admitted slowly, as though the words were being dragged from him by a force he couldn't withstand, 'I don't have anything that was my mother's.'

What was he doing? What was he saying? What was happening to him?

Fear and anger boiled up inside him, but despite that—in direct confrontation of them, in fact—he heard himself continue. 'I wear my father's favourite gold cufflinks for much the same reason, though. He had no formal training, but he was the best deal negotiator I have ever seen. His ability to turn a bad deal round and make it come good was almost magical.'

Why was he telling her this? He had never, ever talked to anyone like this, and could hardly believe that he was doing so now.

'It's obviously a skill that you've inherited from him,' Laura said truthfully, pausing before adding softly, 'I'm sorry that you don't have anything of your mother's to remember her by. You do have her love, though, and a mother's love transcends death.'

Vasilii looked at her, overwhelmed by a need to reach out to her and for her, to hold her and go on holding her, to tell her all those things he had never told anyone else.

She looked so passionately intense, with her eyes bright and her lips flushed and parted, and all he wanted to do was take her in his arms and kiss her until she kissed him back and went on kissing him.

What in damnation was happening to him?

He had to put some distance between them so that he could get himself back to normal. 'We'd better call it a night. We've got an early start in the morning,' he told Laura in a clipped voice.

Out of nowhere inside his head, suddenly and wholly unexpectedly, he could see his mother's face. Her lovely eyes were both tender with her love for him and at the same time reproaching him, in the same way they had done when as a child he had ignored her pleas not to be stubborn and risk hurting himself by doing so.

This was Laura's doing. Somehow she had the power to affect him like this.

'Yes.'

How wooden her own voice sounded, Laura recognised. Would Vasilii hear in it her longing to prolong their conversation and to keep him close to her?

Determined not to let him guess how she really felt, she started to turn away from him, saying as she did so, 'Shall I use the bathroom first or…?'

She was going to walk away from him, and once she had…

There was no place in his life for a woman like Laura—a woman who would want commitment and all the things that went with that. He should just let her go. Letting her go was the right thing to do. So why was he walking towards her, his voice raw with longing as he said her name as though it was a prayer?

Laura trembled as she stood and waited for Vasilii to reach her. Unbelievably, he was going to kiss her. She could see it in his eyes—sense it in the way he looked at her mouth. A clarion call of wild, excited joy pealed through her.

Vasilii lifted his hand as though to cup the side of her face and then dropped it again, shaking his head as he said harshly, 'No!'

It was too much for Laura to endure.

'Yes,' she insisted, finding a courage she had never known she had. Her voice grew stronger as she repeated, '*Yes*,' and then put her own hand on Vasilii's shoulder as she leaned towards him.

Silently they looked at one another—Laura quivering from head to foot in a mixture of wariness and longing, Vasilii's eyes darkening with quickening male need—and then he was kissing her, fiercely and passionately, making the whole of her thrill to the desire she could sense in him as well as to the desire he was arousing within her. His hand cupped her breast, shaping its softness, his thumb brushing against her nipple, slowly, rhythmically, hypnotically, until she was breathing in time to the rhythm of his touch.

It was as though the whole of his self-control had been blasted away from him, Vasilii recognised as he took Laura's mouth in a searingly, sensually intense kiss. Somewhere outside the need that was demolishing his self-control Vasilii was aware of a terse inner voice, demanding to know what he thought he was doing. The same inner voice was warning him that his behaviour was reckless, that it was dangerous, that it went against everything he had ever planned for himself. But the sound of that voice was so distant and vague that it couldn't compete with the crashing, surging, leaping urgency of the force that had take possession of him. He should stop. He wanted to stop. But the plain truth was that he couldn't. He wanted her too much. That wanting was an agony inside him, brought to life by the feel of her in his arms and the taste of her on his lips, savaging him, possessing him, storming through him and allowing nothing to stand in its way.

She should stop him, Laura knew. If she didn't she would regret it. He would reject her, just as he had already done once, and she would be humiliated again. She must stop him now—whilst she still could. She tried to pull away, but the insistent possession of Vasilii's tongue was tempting her lips to open for him, just as the equally demanding thrust of his thigh between her own was causing them not just to part but to cling to the hard, muscular masculinity of him in mute welcome.

It was too late. She couldn't stop him because she couldn't stop herself, Laura recognised. Everything she had felt in his arms before she was feeling again right now—only this time every one of those sensations, every one of those aching pulses of female desire, was intensified a hundredfold—or so it seemed to her—as her longing for him flooded through her, submerging the last of her resistance.

Had he really realised before how much he wanted her? Vasilii wondered. Had he really recognised the intensity of the fierce pleasure there was in simply owning that need? Letting it surge through him? Giving in to it and all that it meant? Finally admitting that from the minute he had seen her it had been inevitable that he would finally give in to the desire she aroused within him?

Every breath she took, every tiny shudder she gave, every small movement she made added to the heat of his own need. Feeling, seeing, caressing the sweet rose-dark hardness of her nipples and hearing her cry out in wild pleasure filled him with an unfamiliar male satisfaction at his ability to conjure such a reckless need from her. He wanted her to lose her self-control, because he knew how close he was to losing his own, Vasilii recognised, and he slid her clothing from her body and clothed it instead with his own touch: shaping her breasts, tugging with his mouth in hot sensual pleasure on one nipple whilst he drew an equal measure of erotic sensation with his fingers and thumb on the other.

She couldn't stand this. She would fragment into a hundred thousand tiny pieces if she had to bear any more of it, Laura thought frantically. Her body was simply not capable of holding so much sensual arousal. She felt as though the intensity of it was going to spill out of her—as though neither her senses nor her flesh could contain it. And yet still the need continued to build inside her.

Somehow, without the need for words, clothes were removed and discarded. On their way to the waiting bed, Laura felt her whole body shuddering with agonised emotion when Vasilii slowly and carefully removed her earrings and placed them safely to one side. For that tenderness alone she could have loved him. *Loved* him? Laura wanted to cling to the safety of denial but it was too late. She was being swept away in the tsunami of emotions and sensations that was rushing through her.

Vasilii kissed her throat and her collarbone, and then the aching longing of her breasts, where her nipples almost hurt with the violence of their need to feel the demanding heat of his mouth taking that need and replacing it with shudder-inducing waves of frantic pleasure that crashed down on her. The girl she had been had never dreamed of pleasure like this—a woman's pleasure and a woman's desire for the one man who could seize and satisfy that desire.

Vasilii's hand slipped between her legs, his touch drawing a low cry of torment from her when he cupped her sex. The soft mound was swollen, proud with the desire she wanted him to know he had aroused in her. His hand stroked her more intimately, and the physical response that gripped her shafted through her, making her cry out in fierce need. She felt as though her whole body was convulsing around the place where he was caressing her—as though every sensation she could ever possess was focused on that one small place. She wanted him to stop. She wanted him never to stop. But he did stop, and her aching body pulsed with a fierce need that dominated all her senses.

Her sweet warmth and wetness were inciting him to finish what he had begun, but some deep-rooted instinct was overpowering his immediate hot need, telling him that this time—with this woman, with Laura—for the first time his overriding and most important need must be to put her pleasure and satisfaction before his own, and that doing so would be his pleasure and satisfaction.

Laura, for her part, could only look up at Vasilii as he shaped her naked body first with his hands and then with his lips, until she was writhing helplessly beneath the torment of this slow-building unstoppable tide of rising desire. Moans of helpless pleasure were drawn from her throat in response to the agony of desire Vasilii was drawing from her body. She tried to reach for him, wanting to caress him as intimately as he was her, wanting to stroke and hold and *know* the male fullness of him, but as her fingertips grazed his erection he pulled back from her on a harsh raw groan that shuddered through his body.

'You don't want me to touch you?' The betraying words were said before she could stop them, but even more shockingly intimate than that betrayal was Vasilii's savage admission.

'I want it too much. If you touch me now…'

He was arching over her, bending his head to kiss her, the strain visible in the cording of his muscles. The temptation was too much for

Laura. She ran her hands over his shoulders and then down his back, before stroking the flat hollow plane of his belly with her fingertips. His kiss became a hot, demanding meshing of lips and mouths and tongues, almost a battle that they were fighting for control of the wild sensuality they had both unleashed.

Laura's hand closed round Vasilii's erection, stroking the hot silken flesh. Her own body shuddered in the wild fire of female delight at his maleness. And then Vasilii was removing her hand, and that hot silken male flesh was sliding against her waiting wetness, thrusting powerfully into the trembling eagerness of her own sex. Frantically Laura rose up to meet him, her body opening to him, her muscles wrapping around him in a silent, mindless female paean of joy.

The barrier was there—its very existence challenging something primitively male within him that Vasilii had never imagined he possessed. His body clamoured for possession of Laura's. One more thrust, careful but deep and slow, and he was there. The barrier was gone and the sound of Laura's soft cry of arousal was reverberating inside his head as she clung to him, whispering to him not to hesitate or stop, not to deny her what she most wanted. What *he* most wanted, Vasilii recognised as he felt the sweet tightness of her muscles clinging to him as she moved urgently and rhythmically against him, inciting him to drive deeper, harder, showing her flesh his rhythm, compelling it to move in time to it.

Oh, but this was so much more than she had ever imagined. A pleasure drawn in every colour heaven could produce when she had previously imagined it in what she now recognised as colourless, insipid shades of grey.

The movement of Vasilii's body within her own was driving her, taking her onwards and upwards, each quickening thrust flooding her with fresh pleasure and increased urgency— until suddenly she was there, and her body was convulsing around Vasilii's in wave after wave of a pleasure so intense that she cried out at the enormity of it. She clung desperately to Vasilii for strength and safety as it filled her and possessed her, her sobbed cry of release mingling with the harsh sound of triumph made by Vasilii just before she felt the hot male pulse of his own release within her.

In a stillness that was racked by the exhausted sound of their breathing, Laura felt Vasilii withdraw from her. The most intense and painful feeling of grief and loss filled her. She was going to cry, she knew. She mustn't let Vasilii see her tears. She knew that rationally he had not wanted to make love to her, and that he would find some way of rejecting her and telling her that it had meant nothing. She knew that. But right now she simply wasn't strong enough to cope with it. All she wanted to do was hide herself away from him—to protect herself and her pain from him. Because that pain meant that she…

That she what? That she loved him? No. It simply meant that right now she was very vulnerable, she assured herself, and she moved away from Vasilii, turning on her side with her back to him as she crept as close to the edge of the bed as she could.

Vasilii frowned as he looked at Laura's back. She should be in his arms. She should be telling him in a soft voice shaken with pleasure and delight how well he had pleasured her, not lying silently as far away from him as she could.

Was she regretting what had happened? Did she wish that it had been her precious John to whom she had given herself?

The feeling that ripped through him was so unfamiliar that it took Vasilii several seconds to recognise it for what it was. Jealousy. He was filled with jealousy at the thought that Laura might have preferred someone else to be her first lover—and he was gripped by a mixture of anger and something that he was forced to recognise as actual pain because she hadn't shown him the post-sex tenderness he had anticipated. Because she hadn't curled up against him and whispered emotionally that their lovemaking had been wonderful, that *he* had been wonderful and that she...

That she what? That she loved him?

He wanted Laura to *love* him?

No. He didn't want anyone to love him. Someone who loved him—especially someone like Laura—would want him to love her back, and he could not do that. Not ever. Loving someone meant worrying about losing them, about them disappearing from his life just as his mother had done.

No, he did not want Laura to love him.

So why did his arms feel so empty? Why did he have this compulsion to reach out to her and draw her close to him and keep her there? Why did the prospect of his life seem so empty if she wasn't in it with him?

CHAPTER ELEVEN

THEY had spent the morning being shown round the very impressive winery, and then after lunch Wu Ying's cousin and Vasilii had sat down together to go through the paper form of the contract before signing it. Now they had just completed a tour of one of the trading ports originally set up by the British, and they were on their way back to their transport to take them back to the château. By rights his only feeling should be one of triumph, Vasilii acknowledged, returning Wu Ying's smile as she left her cousin's side to walk closer to him.

'You and Laura have had a fall-out? Only I have noticed how distant you have been with one another today.'

What Wu Ying meant was that Laura was being distant with *him*. Apart from performing her translation duties she had barely looked at him, never mind spoken to him, and now—although she was at his side—there was at least a metre between them. It was his pride that didn't like Wu Ying's question, and pride, too, that made him close that gap and put his arm round Laura's shoulders, drawing her immediately tense body closer to his own as he answered Wu Ying.

'No, we haven't had a fall-out. Laura always insists on behaving very professionally when we are working together.'

At Vasilii's side, Laura took the hint she knew Vasilii was giving her, reminding her that in Wu Ying's eyes they were supposed to be lovers and a couple. The tension gripping her body just because Vasilii was holding her made her feel as though she might crack apart with the unbearable pain of being so close to him whilst knowing that she meant nothing to him. After the intimacy they had shared, knowing it was a hundred times harder to bear than it had been before. Now she also had to bear the knowledge that the act of possession which had meant so much to her had meant nothing to him. Silent tears she hadn't been able to control had soaked her pillow last night, but thankfully she had managed to protect herself from the humiliation she would have felt had Vasilii known about them.

She couldn't wait to get back to London. They were leaving this evening, so thankfully she would be spared another night in that bed where she had given her body and her love to Vasilii. In return he had given her the greatest physical pleasure she would ever know and the most intense emotional pain she would ever have.

Love. There—finally she had admitted it. Against all reason and logic, against everything she had thought she knew about herself, somehow—ridiculously, foolishly, damagingly—she had fallen in love with the real Vasilii. With a complex, proud, demanding, arrogant alpha male. In short with everything that Vasilii was. Why? She had no idea—no explanation for a folly that she knew could only hurt her. She just had. And now she wanted to get back to London, so that she could put some proper physical distance between them ahead of the time when his real PA returned to work. Then she could put a permanent and complete distance between them.

It had occurred to her whilst they had been in China that there might be an opening for her skills here, and she had decided to try to keep in touch with Wu Ying in the hope of enlisting her support should she decide to relocate here.

Vasilii was still holding her. She could feel him looking at her, his gaze demanding that she look back at him. She didn't want to. She was afraid of what he might see in her eyes. But she couldn't stop herself.

He was smiling down at her, looking at her with a gaze that she knew that Wu Ying would interpret as one of tenderness mixed with desire. Her own body was interpreting it as such. Right now her body wanted to lean even more closely into him and wrap its arms around him, whilst she lifted her face to his for his kiss. Her body was even more of a fool than her heart. Vasilii was simply role-playing—being the tender lover Wu Ying wanted to believe he was to back up her own judgement. It was a relief to Laura that they were now so close to their transport that she could pull away from him and get into the car via the door the driver was holding open for her.

The long stretch limousine was more than large enough for four. It was a very definite sign of how highly Wu Ying's cousin rated Vasilii that he travelled with them, leaving his officials to travel in the other cars behind theirs. Laura was, of course, delighted that Vasilii had secured his contract. She needed the bonus he had promised her, after all. And she needed her time with him to be brought to a speedy end. Better the short, sharp pain of a single blow to separate her from him than the agony of suffering a thousand cuts that came from being in his presence and being ignored by him.

Back at the château, Laura went up to their room to prepare for their onward journey, whilst Vasilii was borne off by Wu Ying and her cousin for a final discussion about the contract. In the tower room Laura showered quickly, with one eye on the locked door to the bathroom, telling herself that her heart was pumping so fast because she was dreading the thought of Vasilii returning before she was out of the shower, dried off and back in her clothes.

So why was she now lingering under its pulsing spray? Why was she soaping herself so dreamily? Why was she tempted to go and unlock that door in the hope that Vasilii would return and find her here, naked, eager, wanting him?

A sound that was somewhere between an aching moan of need and a stifled sob of self-contempt left her throat raw with the torment of her own emotions. To punish herself she stepped out of the shower, rubbing her body dry quickly and briskly before wrapping a fresh towel around herself and then going into the dressing room. She also locked the door there as she changed into the fresh clothes she had put to one side for their journey back to Heathrow.

Their cases had already been packed for them

and removed, and once dressed she waited for Vasilii, taking the opportunity to double-check the wardrobe and the cupboards to ensure that nothing had been left behind.

She had just finished doing so when Vasilii walked into the room.

He was frowning heavily, avoiding looking at her as he strode over to the tall narrow window. Now that they were on their own and there was no need for him to put on a show for Wu Ying he did not want to look at her, she knew. He did not want to have anything whatsoever to do with her. He no doubt wanted to forget that last night had ever happened. In fact from his point of view Laura did not know why it *had* happened. Maybe the unpleasant reality was quite simply that he had just wanted a woman, and the relief of sex, and she had happened to be there.

Vasilii swung round and looked at Laura at last. She was standing with her back to him—so that she didn't have to look at him, of course. She hadn't said a word about last night. No doubt because she was still harbouring a wish that he had been John.

Well, he hadn't. They had made love. She had been a virgin. He had acquired her most valuable bargaining asset—at least in her eyes—and, perhaps most importantly of all, for the first time in his life he had omitted to take any precautions. Healthwise he had no concerns. How could he have? He knew the state of his own sexual health, and he knew that he had been Laura's first lover. But there was something else that could result from unprotected sex.

A child.

A child that would be *his* child.

He knew immediately and without any kind of doubt that such a child must be brought up under his roof and with his name, and that he of all men could never and would never deprive it of its mother. A child who, like its mother, it was his duty to protect. The traditional values of his mother's people were important to Vasilii because they were a part of her. And those values meant that a man had certain responsibilities to a woman's virtue, to any child he fathered. The fact that he could not and would not turn his back on them came as no real surprise to Vasilii.

And his willingness? Indeed his eagerness to perform his duty? Was that also no real surprise to him? Had he already known deep within himself that, no matter what logic told him, where Laura was concerned there was a deeper, stronger power at work inside him whose needs could not be denied? After all, he had known that she was a virgin, and he had known that by taking her virginity he was giving himself no alternative but to do what he must do, hadn't he?

He looked at Laura's stiff back and began to speak in what he hoped was a calm voice that did not betray the intensity of the emotion and the desperation he was really feeling. 'In view of what happened last night I've decided that it would be as well if we got married—and the sooner the better.'

Laura couldn't believe her ears. She turned round slowly.

Just for a handful of seconds she allowed herself to believe. She could almost taste and feel what would be joyful happiness. Vasilii her husband…the children they would have…the family life they would create together, filled with love and laughter and security.

And then Vasilii continued. 'We don't have any alternative. You were a virgin. You could have conceived my child. The ways of my mother's people insist that a man who takes a woman's virginity must marry her to protect her virtue and the child they might have together. I am enough my mother's son to know that even in this modern day and age I cannot go against the traditions of her tribe.'

There was a terrible pain inside Laura's chest

where her heart was—an aching agony of despair. So this was what it felt like to be offered something that looked exactly like what your heart most wanted, but which was in reality a cruel fake, a hollow emptiness. No—worse than that—a terribly destructive proposition that, if accepted, would destroy her self-respect and her sense of self, leaving her with nothing but self-hatred and self-loathing.

From somewhere she found the courage to look at him, her eyes smoky with the intensity of her emotions.

'*Marry* you? Marry a man who doesn't love me? A man who feels he has to marry me out of a sense of duty? A man who doesn't respect or even like me and who certainly doesn't love me? A man who thinks I kept my virginity to use as a bargaining tool for exactly the kind of marriage he's offering me? A marriage into which he feels trapped by his honour whilst refusing me the right to my own sense of honour? No.'

No? Laura was turning him down? The feelings of despair and pain that filled him far outweighed any logical outrage he might be feeling. Only now, when she had turned him down and rejected him, was Vasilii able to admit to himself exactly how much he wanted her as his wife.

'There could be a child,' he reminded her. 'My child.'

'*My* child!' Laura defied him. A child…Vasilii's child. She hadn't even got as far as thinking about that, but of course he was right. Vasilii's child growing inside her. Vasilii's child to cherish and love. The feeling that surged through her told her how much she actually hoped that it might be. But if there was to be a child then that gave her even more reason not to marry him.

'If there is a child then I will deal with that situation,' she told him fiercely. 'I won't allow my child to be brought up within the kind of marriage that ours would be, Vasilii, with its parents neither loving nor respecting one another, with the place where the heart of a family should be cold and empty of all those things that a child needs so much.'

Someone was knocking on their bedroom door. Glad of an excuse not to continue their conversation, in case Vasilii continued to pressure her and she became weak enough to give in, Laura went to open it.

The major-domo was standing outside.

'Your car is waiting for you,' he told her.

Laura nodded her head and thanked him

It was time for them to leave, and with Wu Ying accompanying them to the airport thankfully there would not be any further opportunity for Vasilii to try and break her down, to compel her to agree to a marriage that she knew would destroy her.

CHAPTER TWELVE

IN HIS service apartment Vasilii looked unseeingly at the letters stacked neatly on his desk. By rights he should be going through them— just as he should be lodging the contract he had brought back with his lawyers.

Laura's response to his proposal had stunned him. Stunned him and filled him with a fierce pride in her and an even greater respect for her, as well as increasing his determination to make her his wife, Vasilii admitted. He'd realised, listening to her, that he didn't just love her, he admired her and—despite what she thought— liked her as well.

He had to see her, make her see sense. Surely she would never be able to hold out against the lure of the benefits—the love and the security— that together they could give their child? Like him, she knew the pain of growing up without both parents. She wouldn't want that for their child any more than he did himself. Like him, she'd fight for that not to happen. He'd need an excuse before she'd let him into her apartment, though. Her bonus cheque. That should do it. Her bonus cheque and…

The exclusive international jewellers he contacted were immediately understanding and obliging. Within half an hour of telephoning them Vasilii was in possession of several sample engagement rings and some unset diamonds.

Having let the courier who had delivered them out of the apartment, he was just looking at the stones in their velvet padded box when the door to his office opened and his half-sister Alena walked in.

'You're back!' she exclaimed delightedly. 'Kiryl has a business meeting in the hotel lobby, so I thought I'd come up here and just check that everything's okay.'

Her gaze dropped to the diamonds.

'Those are engagement rings,' she accused him.

'Yes,' Vasilii acknowledged.

Her eyes widening with excitement she demanded, 'You're getting engaged? Vasilii, who *is* she?'

'Laura Westcotte,' Vasilii answered her.

Laura Westcotte. A guilty flush immediately stained Alena's face. She bit her bottom lip and then gave a small shrug. 'This is so silly. I'm a married woman now, but I still sometimes feel like a naughty schoolgirl around you, Vasilii. She will have told you, of course, that what I said about her going off to New York instead of standing in for her aunt and keeping an eye on me wasn't true. I was too much of a coward to tell you at the time. I was delighted when I learned that she'd already left for New York because it meant that I could have some real freedom. It was easy to let you work yourself up into a fury over her supposed selfishness in refusing to help her aunt out. Oh, dear. Is she very cross with me? I do hope not. I remember her from school, of course, and I always admired her. She was so brilliantly clever, and kind—and now she's going to be my sister-in-law.'

Laura *hadn't* behaved irresponsibly towards his half-sister. He had misjudged her—and badly. Normally Vasilii hated the mere thought of being wrong-footed. So why, instead of feeling chagrined, was he actually feeling delighted that he now had another reason to seek Laura out?—that reason being the delivery of an apology. Did he really need to ask himself?

If Alena was surprised when he abruptly announced that he had to go out thankfully she didn't say so, or ask him any questions, or seek to delay him. But then Alena knew what it was to be passionately in love.

It would have been easier, faster, to take the tube to that part of London where Laura lived—but Vasilii had chosen to drive himself instead. After he had persuaded Laura to accept his proposal then he wanted to take her out to dinner. He wanted to show her the love and the esteem he genuinely felt for her. And then he wanted to take her to bed—if she would allow him to—and show her all over again just what his feelings for her really were. She might not love him yet, but she would love their child. And through that child surely she could come to love him, its father?

Laura sat down on the small sofa in her sitting room, but then got up again and started to pace the floor. Since arriving home she'd found she couldn't settle—couldn't relax—couldn't do anything other than go over and over Vasilii's proposal to her.

He had tried to restart his argument again on the plane, but Laura had told him that she didn't want to talk about it any more and to her relief he had respected that. To her relief? But wasn't it true that a tiny, treacherous, weak and vulnerable part of her had actually *wanted* him to break down her opposition?

In an attempt to distract herself from her turbulent thoughts, Laura dragged her unopened suitcases in from the hallway and began unpacking, removing her own clothes and other belongings. The rest—her working wardrobe—was going back to Vasilii. Now that she would be working in London she was hardly likely to need it. She placed her mother's jewellery box on the coffee table and beside it the small open box containing her three earrings. When she left Vasilii's employ she would send him back the earring he had had made for her. She knew that she wouldn't be able to bear to keep it.

But what if there *was* a child—a daughter? Wouldn't that solitary earring be something of her father's that could be a precious keepsake for her?

She'd just finished unpacking when the doorbell rang. Laura went to answer it, wondering who on earth it could be. She certainly wasn't expecting anyone.

And she most certainly was not expecting the person that it was—the person striding formidably into her home and filling the small enclosed space of her tiny hallway.

Vasilii.

'I need to talk to you,' he told her promptly.

'I don't want to talk to you,' Laura defied

him. 'Unless what you want to talk to me about is work.'

Vasilii managed a dismissive shrug as he reached past Laura to push open the door to her sitting room.

'I've brought you your bonus cheque. Of course if you don't want it…'

How much she wished that she could deny that she did, but amongst the letters waiting for her return had been one from her aunt's sheltered accommodation, stating that the monthly fees for her room were going up.

'I've also brought you an apology, which I hope you will accept. My half-sister has just informed me that, far from refusing to standing in for your aunt, you were never asked to do so. I misjudged you—I apologise.'

Vindicated. But that vindication didn't bring any sense of satisfaction, Laura recognised.

Vasilii was reaching into his jacket pocket, from which he removed an envelope and then a dark leather box.

'This is your bonus cheque,' he told her. 'And this…' he tapped the box '…this is a selection of engagement rings and stones, one of which I want you to choose for your engagement ring, Laura.'

'I can't marry you.'

'Yes, you can. John—your mentor—I know

you had hoped… But I am wealthier by far than he will ever be, Laura.'

'Money? Do you think that matters to me? What I want from marriage is a man who loves me and whom I love in return. That is the only wealth I desire, Vasilii. And you are *still* misjudging me. When I told you that John was no more than a very good and kind friend to me that was the truth. It remains the truth.'

Vasilii had opened the leather box, and the flash of the diamonds within it was making her blink. Quickly she turned away from them.

'Diamonds don't tempt me, Vasilii.'

'Then what would?'

Was that really a husky note of pleading in his voice? It couldn't be. She had to be imagining it.

The real answer to his question was, of course, *him*—his love, his emotional need for her and commitment to her.

'You could never give me what I most want,' she told him truthfully.

'I may already have given you my child.'

'And I have said that if you have then I will take on the full responsibility for that child.'

'I won't let you.'

'You can't stop me.'

They were glaring at one another now—two adversaries again.

Desperate to put some distance between them, Laura moved away from him—and then wondered what Vasilii was staring at with such frowning intent as he looked past her. Turning her head, she saw the open box containing the three earrings. Instinctively she snatched up the box. She could have scored points off him and even humiliated him a little by letting him know she *knew* he had gone to the trouble of having a new earring made for her—an act of real emotional weakness from a man who prided himself on not having any emotions at all—but stupidly, because she loved him, she wanted to protect him.

'There are three earrings in that box,' Vasilii told her.

Laura's heart turned over inside her chest. She hadn't been quite quick enough and he had seen the earrings.

'Yes,' she was forced to agree.

He was looking at her, watching her. Waiting… Waiting for an explanation she did not want to give him—for his pride's sake. She knew he would hate being revealed as a man who was capable of what he would see as the weakness of compassion—especially to her. Whilst for her what he would see as vulnerability within himself only made her love him all the more.

She took a deep breath. 'The three are the one I was wearing, the one that fell off into the neck of my dress on the plane and the one you told me your pilot had been handed when the plane was cleaned. I didn't say anything earlier because...because I didn't think I could find the words to tell you how grateful I was—am—to you for your kindness and...and how much it meant—means—to me that you would be so thoughtful.' There—she had done it. She had let him see something of what she felt. And for his sake, not her own.

They looked at one another.

Vasilii exhaled the tension from his chest. Laura's honesty demanded that he was equally honest in return. And wasn't it the truth that now, knowing of his love for her, he wanted to tell her why he had done what he had done? He wanted her to know that his action had been motivated by his feelings for her, even if at the time he would have sworn that it wasn't either true or possible.

'I could see how much the earrings meant to you because they'd been your mother's.' He paused. Even now, knowing that he loved her, knowing that he could trust her with whatever he might say to her, he was struggling. A lifetime of denying his feelings, rejecting them and rejecting everything they meant, had seen to that.

'I do know how that feels,' Vasilii continued. 'The last time I saw my mother she was
wearing a pair of gold earrings. Gold filigree
hoops—a traditional pair that came from her
family's tribe.'

This was so hard for him. Laura could see
that. Her heart ached with love for him. She
suspected that he was trying to express the feelings of pain and loss he had carried inside him
for a very long time. She could sense that pain
buried deep inside him, like a sharp sliver of
glass that still hurt. She longed to go to him and
hold him, comfort him, but a deep inbuilt female wisdom urged her to just wait and listen.

'I remember watching her put them on.' Vasilii's words came slowly and with difficulty, as
though just speaking them was a tremendous
effort of will. 'She was going out to dinner,
with some friends. My father was away and I
didn't want her to go. That was the night she
was kidnapped. When her body was found the
earrings were missing. They were never recov-
ered. I swore after my mother's death that I
would never allow myself to become dependent
on someone's love—on someone being there
for me ever again—because losing that love,
losing that person hurt too much.'

So *that* was the root cause of his determination to push people away from him. A child's pain—not an adult man's cruelty.

He had been seven years old—a child, a little boy—desperately longing for the mother he had lost: a boy who had grown up afraid to love again because of that pain.

'Oh, Vasilii.' Without meaning to do so Laura stepped towards him, her heart pierced with the sadness she felt at his obvious pain.

But Vasilii stepped back from her, so that the hand she had extended to touch him met only empty air. Automatically, feeling rejected, Laura stepped back herself—and bumped into the coffee table. It was a bad habit she seemed to have developed around Vasilii, she acknowledged, and she turned round just in time to see her precious jewellery box sliding towards the edge of the table.

They both moved together, but Vasilii was faster. As he gathered up the box his thumb somehow pressed the spring that opened the secret drawer as he gripped it.

'I'll take it.' Swiftly Laura reached for the box, trying not to panic. Why, oh, why had she not thrown away that incriminating photograph?

She was holding out her hands for the box. She had even dared to brave the private space Vasilii liked to keep around himself by stepping into it. And for once he hadn't reacted by stepping back from her. Because he was staring down into the open drawer. Because he was removing the two halves of her photograph—*his* photograph. Because he was patching them together and looking at them. And now he was looking at her with one eyebrow raised questioningly.

There was no escape. Laura knew that.

'I took it from my bedroom window at school. You'd just dropped off your sister.' She gave a small shrug. 'I was the orphaned niece of the school's matron—a charity case, given education at the school because of my aunt's position. And because of that position she could never be seen to favour or indulge me, so my life tended to be rather lonely. I didn't have the kind of moneyed family background that would have enabled me to fit in with the other girls— school trips, visiting one another's homes, that kind of thing. When I saw the loving way you were with your sister, I felt so envious of her. She had parents who loved her. She had a protective brother whom she clearly adored, who was prepared to spoil and indulge her by driving her to school in his obviously new and very glamorous car. I don't know why I took that photograph, except that for me what I saw represented something I could never have.'

That at least was true, Laura recognised.

She couldn't tell from the way Vasilii was looking at her whether or not he had accepted her explanation or what he was thinking about it. Was he pitying her? Feeling compassion for her? Contempt for her…?

However, when he began to speak, his opening words were such a shock that they caused her own thoughts to spin dizzily and fearfully out of control—because what he was saying was nothing like what she had imagined he would say.

'I was right when I stated that there must have been a reason why you remained a virgin,' he said slowly, and then stopped. He was having trouble controlling not just the delivery and the pace of what he knew would be the most important words he would ever say in the whole of his life, he was also having trouble in controlling the breath he needed to say them.

The reality was that he didn't want to waste time in speech. What he wanted to do was to take Laura in his arms and hold her and kiss her until she admitted to him that she loved him. Vasilii knew now that she did—or at least that she felt enough for him to be able to tenderly cherish that existing flame of pure emotion into a love for him that he knew could be encouraged to burn within her for the rest of their shared lives.

'This photograph…' he continued.

But Laura shook her head to stop him. He was getting too close to where she was so very vulnerable. Far too close—and it was too painful.

'I *was* right when I said that you'd had a hidden agenda for keeping your virginity,' he repeated. 'For maybe a woman who had fallen in love very young, given her heart to a man she could not have, might remain a virgin.'

Laura didn't pretend not to understand him. There wasn't any point. Not now.

'I was girl—a teenager. The Vasilii I fell head over heels in love with didn't exist—had never existed and never could exist—so it was no wonder that I never met a man who could match up to that foolish ideal.'

'But you gave yourself to *me*—to this Vasilii,' he pointed out. 'You cried out my name in your pleasure. You—'

'I will *not* love a man who has already told me that he can never love me back.' Laura stopped him, unable to bear any more. 'I cannot.'

Because it would destroy her. It was already destroying her. Marriage to Vasilii would be a pitiless, merciless descent to a place where she would give herself over to a hope that would ultimately crush the life from her heart and bring her only pain.

'I lied,' Vasilii told her quietly.

Two simple words, but said with such sincerity and truth, such strength and intent, that they had the power to smash down barriers and create out of the dust a shimmering place of hope and belief.

Laura looked at him and waited. The next move had to come from him.

And miraculously, cleansingly, it did. 'I love you, Laura,' he told her firmly. 'I think I knew that you had the power to command love from me right from the start, but—predictably, I suppose—I fought against that knowledge because I was afraid of what it meant. I was afraid of loving you. The night we made love, though—when you turned your back on me I wanted so much to hold you and keep you to me. I wanted to hear you say that you cared about me…that you were glad it had been me… that you had wanted me. I knew then what my real feelings for you were. I want us to marry because quite simply my life will be empty without you. I thought the worst pain I could ever know was losing the person I loved. I know now that the worst pain of all would be never being able to tell that person that I love them. Never being able to hear them say back to me that they love me.'

As he spoke Vasilii closed the distance between them, his movements towards her strong and sure—the action of an alpha man. *Her* man, Laura acknowledged, and she let him take her in his arms, let him kiss her, woo her, with the sweetest and most tender of lover's kisses as he covered her lips with his own. Slowly and deliberately he caressed them into willing compliance with the desire he was inciting within her, so that within seconds she was clinging to him, and returning the increasing passion of his kisses with her own.

'I love you, Laura, and there is nothing in this life that is more important to me than having you love me back willingly, happily, and knowing that from now on your trust in me, your love for me, will be the most precious things I have.'

'I *do* love you,' Laura admitted. 'I didn't want to, but I do. I love you, Vasilii. Not the one-dimensional romantic fantasy of my girlish dreams, but the real man—the real Vasilii.'

'Whatever you want I will give you, Laura.'

'Whatever I want?' she questioned him.

'Yes.'

'All I want is your love, Vasilii. Your love, and for you to take me to bed—right now, please.'

'You do not need to ask. I am the one who

should be begging you to allow me the pleasure of loving you.'

He couldn't say any more because Laura was putting her arms around him, her mouth on his, whispering that she wanted him to show her how much he loved her.

Their lovemaking was intense and passionate—a physical and emotional commitment to one another so special and so private, with so many promises given and healing words exchanged—that at the end of it, when they lay together in the post-coital calm of one another's arms, it was Laura who gently kissed away the traces of Vasilii's emotional tears from his damp eyelashes. Her heart was filled past bursting with love and pride for this wonderful man who had grown so much through his love for her that he was willingly letting her see his vulnerability.

EPILOGUE

'YOU are such a darling for being so understanding about that lie I told Vasilii,' Alena told
Laura as she stood at Laura's side on the church
steps in her role as Laura's matron of honour.

They were both waiting for Vasilii to finish
thanking the minister who had married them
at a pretty church in the small village close to
the school where Laura had first seen him. It
had been the most wonderful day—a simple,
traditional service, attended by Vasilii's half-
sister and her husband, Kiryl, as well as Laura's
aunt and their closest friends.

Amongst the guests was Wu Ying, along with
her husband, and Laura had been delighted to
see how much happier and closer the Chinese
couple seemed.

Alena went to join her husband and Vasilii
turned back to her, taking hold of her hand and
raising it to his lips to brush a tender but discreet kiss across the back of her knuckles.

'It's been a wonderful day,' Laura told him.

'But you are sad because there are people special to us who are missing?' Vasilii guessed, perfectly understanding the reason for the small shadow that momentarily darkened her gaze.

'Our parents,' Laura agreed.

'They are here, my darling wife. I am sure of it. They are here with us and happy for us, even though we cannot see them. Love is a very powerful force, and what I have learned through my love for you tells me that the love our parents had for us won't have died. It is still here—with us and for us.'

'Yes,' Laura agreed. 'Yes, you are right.'

The look she was giving him was causing Vasilii to tense his body against the sudden fierce flood of desire that surged over him.

'If you keep looking at me like that we're going to be the first bride and groom on record who don't make it to their own wedding breakfast because the groom is too busy making love to his bride and showing her just how much he loves her. You have changed my life, Laura. You have shown me what real love is. I want to spend the rest of my life showing you how much you mean to me.'

She was trembling, Laura recognised. Trembling with joy and love, and that same longing to be alone with him, so that they could express their love for one another in the most intimate way possible.

The church bells were ringing, their guests were waiting, and their love was a river of emotion that would carry them together throughout the journey that would be the rest of their lives.

'I love you,' Laura whispered as they headed for their waiting car.

'And I love you, too,' Vasilii said back.

* * * * *

LARGER-PRINT BOOKS!

Harlequin *Presents*

PASSION GUARANTEED SEDUCTION

GET 2 FREE LARGER-PRINT NOVELS PLUS 2 FREE GIFTS!

YES! Please send me 2 FREE LARGER-PRINT Harlequin Presents® novels and my 2 FREE gifts (gifts are worth about $10). After receiving them, if I don't wish to receive any more books, I can return the shipping statement marked "cancel". If I don't cancel, I will receive 6 brand-new novels every month and be billed just $4.80 per book in the U.S. or $5.49 per book in Canada. That's a saving of at least 13% off the cover price! It's quite a bargain! Shipping and handling is just 50¢ per book in the U.S. and 75¢ per book in Canada.* I understand that accepting the 2 free books and gifts places me under no obligation to buy anything. I can always return a shipment and cancel at any time. Even if I never buy another book, the two free books and gifts are mine to keep forever.

176/376 HDN FER2

Name	(PLEASE PRINT)	
Address		Apt. #
City	State/Prov.	Zip/Postal Code

Signature (if under 18, a parent or guardian must sign)

Mail to the **Reader Service:**
IN U.S.A.: P.O. Box 1867, Buffalo, NY 14240-1867
IN CANADA: P.O. Box 609, Fort Erie, Ontario L2A 5X3

Not valid for current subscribers to Harlequin Presents Larger-Print books.

**Are you a subscriber to Harlequin Presents books and want to receive the larger-print edition?
Call 1-800-873-8635 today or visit us at www.ReaderService.com.**

* Terms and prices subject to change without notice. Prices do not include applicable taxes. Sales tax applicable in N.Y. Canadian residents will be charged applicable taxes. Offer not valid in Quebec. This offer is limited to one order per household. All orders subject to credit approval. Credit or debit balances in a customer's account(s) may be offset by any other outstanding balance owed by or to the customer. Please allow 4 to 6 weeks for delivery. Offer available while quantities last.

Your Privacy—The Reader Service is committed to protecting your privacy. Our Privacy Policy is available online at www.ReaderService.com or upon request from the Reader Service.

We make a portion of our mailing list available to reputable third parties that offer products we believe may interest you. If you prefer that we not exchange your name with third parties, or if you wish to clarify or modify your communication preferences, please visit us at www.ReaderService.com/consumerchoice or write to us at Reader Service Preference Service, P.O. Box 9062, Buffalo, NY 14269. Include your complete name and address.

HPLP11B

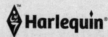